PRUSSIAN BLUE

ZARA KATANZARO

Prussian Blue

Book One of *The Oil Paint Series*

Edited by Manda Waller

Cover illustration by Jonas Špokas of Stardust Book Services

Cover typography by Norman Olasiman of Stardust Book Services

Interior Formatting by Sara Vertuan of Stardust Book Services

eBook ISBN: 978-1-9192895-1-9

Paperback ISBN: 978-1-9192895-0-2

A CIP catalogue record for this title is available from the British Library.

First published in the UK in 2025

Acknowledgements

My first (and biggest) thanks absolutely go to my devoted mum and dad for your true kindness and generosity. Your patience and understanding (especially through my OCD and pre-menstrual madness) transcends this world. Thanks for being my earth angels and teaching me how to fly. You are the kindest souls.

To my eternal boyfriend, for keeping me on track and riding the menopausal waves; for your continuous faith in my journey and accepting my quirks; but most of all, for opening your shutters and pouring in Big Love. Thank you, thank you, thank you.

Bestest Bro, thanks for your encouragement and belief through every stage of my creative life – not just for the book but for all your technological wisdom designing websites and flyers – I know it drove you mad! You have unknowingly inspired us all.

Super Sis, thank you for balancing my mind between the real and ethereal worlds. You infuse exceptional motivation and vision. Thanks for all our holiday laughs and memories. You're an awesome mum!

To everyone who has come and gone in my life, you are the colours of the tapestry.

To JM, thanks for our friendship, never telling me what to do, for always catching my falls, untangling the knots and driving me forward; for our silliness, happiness and everythingness.

To my sincere friends, thanks for all your support emotionally and "bookly." I am blessed that you share your lives with me.

Manda Waller, my editor, thanks for helping me navigate the next part of the book-writing process; you have illuminated the editing world, and your corrections and guidance have been invaluable.

To all the team at Stardust Book Services. Nastasia Bishop-McHugh, Jonas Špokas, Norman Olasiman, Sara Vertuan and Jen Tolnay, thanks for your endless help, advice and easy communication. You have made it real.

Chapter One

Kai wore nothing but Sapphire Blue nail varnish on her toenails and wondered how on earth she got to be standing this side of the easel. Perhaps this was where most artists ended up after six years of studying and ten years of exhibiting.

Naked.

For almost twelve pounds an hour!

"… and you will have the best years of your lives," the professor of Visual Arts had promised the year one students on their first day in that lecture room years ago. Everyone had applauded – and with hindsight, to date, that statement may have been true. But perhaps, to reflect reality, he could have added, "After that, a thousand galleries will reject you … even if they like your artwork. They will judge you personally and smile sickly-snobbishly sweetly, fobbing you off with, "Your paintings are lovely, but …"

1. We're not taking any new artists at the moment. *(Rubbish!)*
2. We already have an artist who paints in a similar style to yours. (Where *exactly?)*

3. Your work is too unique. *(See number 2!)*
4. You're not related to anyone I know. *(Getting closer ...)*
5. I don't like the look of you. *(Bingo!)*

So here she stood, at Wattles Abbey College, in a thirty-minute pose that her former uni tutors would be proud of: head turned to gaze past the left shoulder so her eyes could rest on eight gold drawing pins arranged in a circle on an empty notice board, left hand on hip. Right foot raised on a box with the heel lifted to encourage "accentuation of the calf muscle" *(cramp)* while her right hand dug the famous life-drawing stick upright into the ground, to the outside of her right thigh.

She was itching to see how many more minutes she had left to stand in this position. Her neck was starting to grumble – and no matter how many ways you count eight gold drawing pins arranged in a circle, it doesn't ease the aches or speed up time. If health and safety were visiting, they would shut it down immediately.

At least the fan heater was on!

"Two minutes left." Annika's voice interrupted her thoughts. *Two minutes? Didn't she say that two minutes ago?* Two more minutes meant something completely different being an artist. It signified invaluable observing, measuring and foreshortening. As the life model, it served as one hundred and twenty seconds of disappointment, pain and boredom.

Annika was Russian; a gifted realist painter and completely wasted teaching life and portrait classes. Oh yes, that's right! A *teacher* – you can also become a teacher if the galleries don't like the sound of your surname.

And a teacher Kai was. A swimming instructor of over sixteen years.

She hated every second of it.

Kai wondered if any of these eight mature art students had included the survival scars on her left forearm in their paintings: the keloids perhaps needing a Raw Umber mix, the paler ones more of a Burnt Sienna.

"One more minute."

Oh, you gotta *be kidding?*

The fingers on her right hand were too numb to complain, while her internal subtle energy inconspicuously fell away from the flesh and bones which took credit for continuing to hold the pose, giving nothing away.

Not that she had anywhere more exciting to be. At three o'clock, she would get dressed and head over to Greyton Leisure Centre to teach swimming. If the muscles in her face hadn't given up the will, she'd have frowned at the thought.

"OK, everyone, time's up."

Her shoulders relaxed. She placed her right heel flat on the floor, grimacing at the tightness of her calf as she pointed and flexed her foot and circled the ankle. Gently, she rotated her head towards the right shoulder for a counterpose, producing a burning sensation in her neck.

"Thank you, Kai." Annika smiled as she walked towards the platform, arm extended to take the stick.

"Yes, thanks, Kai," the class chorused. "We always need more time though."

"Ah, you're welcome," Kai fibbed, stepping off the platform and into her pink Spanish loafer slippers, hiding her delight that time could no longer rip her body to shreds. She picked her blue, fluffy dressing gown off the chair and twirled it around her shoulders, tying the belt at the front. They were a respectful group who spoke to her with the same dignity whether her clothes were on or off.

"Come and have a look if you like?"

"Oh. OK, thanks." Kai was pleased they didn't mind her seeing their interpretations of herself. "Wow, these are good."

She was genuinely impressed at their advanced painting styles – and felt a little jealous that she was not maintaining her own life-drawing skills.

Some had made her olive skin a little darker, others a little lighter. Each painted-Kai came with its own character – she wondered who she'd be in each of these eight alternate lives. None of them had scars on their arms.

"Kai?" Annika called her over. "Shall we try and synchronise some dates in the diary for the next few sessions?"

"Sure." She walked to her sports bag piled with swimming paraphernalia and rummaged around for her diary. Mondays and Wednesdays were already blocked out for her sales assistant job at the chemist, so they booked the Tuesday and Thursday for the week after next, and the second week after that. Colleges like to rotate the models, to introduce a variety of shapes and sizes … which was great, because she could then coordinate the dates to miss her heavy menstrual days. She dedicated Fridays and the weekends to channel whatever was hanging around in the ether to manifest onto the canvas.

It was ten to three. She shoved her diary back in the bag, scooped up her clothes, and said goodbye to Annika and the class, who thanked her again.

The stone-cold toilets in the corridor offered their draughty quarters as her changing room. Reluctantly, she allowed the warmth of the dressing gown to escape as she wriggled into her swimming costume and slipped the navy-blue Aertex T-shirt with green trim over her head. She pulled on the oversized navy-blue shorts, stamped her feet into her trainers, swung her sports bag over her left shoulder and headed out to her blue Vauxhall Astra.

Driving through the small affluent village, with small high-street cottages either side (some with thatched roofs but none with parking), Kai wondered why on earth people paid ridiculous money for tiny little boxes with expensive postcodes. If she parked next to the kerb, sat in the passenger seat and wound down the window, she could almost knock on their front doors.

It was three o'clock. She'd be at work in time to set up the floats, noodles and toys to start the first lesson at four p.m. Waving adios to the village in her rear-view mirror, she rumbled along the link road to Greyton, passing endless fields of green and yellow inviting her to stop and lie with them to absorb their colour and energy while watching the clouds. Another expensive area, though the houses here were bigger and had driveways and front gardens to set them away from the road. A few even had swimming pools in their back gardens where she taught private sessions.

She turned left into Greyton Leisure Centre and let the fizz of anxiety in her tummy take over for a few moments. She was preparing herself for The Zoo, as it had come to be named by the swimming teachers. The sign actually read *Viewing Gallery*, but it would have been better off stating *Do Not Feed the Animals*. Oh, and stay away from their young or expect a lot of hissing and spitting. There were always a handful that spoiled it for the rest.

She tapped the dashboard with her right index finger in three places as she slowly inhaled, taking care not to get to the top of the breath before the third tap … that could mean the end of life completely. The first two points were always tapped close together, while the third was placed further along in a direction moving away from her body – to block all the horridness from coming near.

It was a coping strategy that her brain lovingly deceived her into thinking would stop bad things from happening.

But it wasn't just the taps. The space between her thighs had to be right; the way she breathed would change; her shoulders would literally shrug off the intrusion while her shoulder blades drew together, broadening her chest, creating good upper posture. Her eyes would often mirror the sequence of taps, finding a green bush or tree, or the simple sky and just about any other place that could contain the ritual without quickly triggering the mind into another catastrophe.

And if she didn't do it right, she would have to set up the entire alignment again and start from the beginning … in a slightly different space.

She'd had healthy discussions with her therapist, Jane, as to whether it was part of the brain that functioned differently or the mind inventing a catatonic formula to be repeated over and over to prevent the slightest of disasters. Jane favoured the latter; Kai thought it to be a combination of both.

Pulling the key from the ignition, she peeled herself out of the car, gathered her sports bag and threw it over her shoulder.

"Hellooo." A voice came from behind her. It was Charlotte, a swimming teacher in her sixties who had been here for years. She was calm and tranquil.

"Buongiorno!" Kai smiled. "How's you?"

"I'm very well, thank you. Glad to be out of the house and all his moaning. He's sooo miserable."

"Oh dear! Negative Nelly playing up?" Kai knew the story of Charlotte's niggling husband, always moaning and getting under her feet, and wondered why on earth couples stayed together if all they did was gripe about one another.

"Tell me why I'm here again?" Kai asked, hoping to be showered in some magic inspirational dust.

"Ahhh, right … that would be because you have bills to pay, so you can keep your house and buy the things you want." Charlotte's wise voice pinned the words to the air with slow precision.

"Oh yes, that's right …" Kai nodded, conducting her finger along the aired sentence. She fluttered her eyelids down as each word glared at her menacingly with a perverse reassurance. "Because I wasn't sure." They giggled, walked into reception and signed in. But Kai's giggle had been losing its bounce for a while.

There were queues at the desk as usual – kids hanging off metal bars that separated the entrance from the exit, and an exasperated mother trying to stop one of her children running out into the car park while tying the shoelaces of the other. A toddler stood with his older brother at the vending machine, marvelling impatiently as the rotating metal uncoiled and released his packet of Skittles.

Kai didn't have kids. She treasured her travels and afternoon snoozes, but the best part of the day was climbing into bed, sinking the side of her face onto the soft pillow and pulling the covers up to her chin as she drifted off into the land of illusions.

"Right," Charlotte coaxed as they put on the cheap, blue plastic overshoes. "Are we ready?"

"Not really, but let's get it over with."

They were met with the familiar humid, chlorine-scented air that warmed and stifled. The lifeguards would start setting up the lanes for swimming lessons in about ten minutes, and the excited screams and shouts of boys and girls currently in the pool would soon turn to grumbles and groans at having been chucked out. Two lanes would be kept for serious swimmers, who would moan at there not being enough space for a decent workout.

A glass-panelled door led them out of the commotion and into the diving area. The door sighed heavily as they pushed it open, synchronising with the plummet of Kai's heart. They stepped into the diving area where the floor of the square flexi pool had been raised all the way to the top, inviting anyone to wander across it, giving the deception of walking on water. An ingenious invention of a movable floor to accommodate diving off the boards when the floor was lowered to its maximum depth of four metres; or to support beginners' swimming lessons until they were ready to move into the main pool.

Although the journey to the other side of the pool was a lot quicker across the diagonal when the floor was all the way to the top, Kai decided against it this time, remembering the lack of traction with her trainers on the slippery surface and a comical back-jarring, hip-thrusting slide from one end to the other. *How do eighteen-year-old boys make it look so easy?*

She placed her bag down by the huge glass wall with a view across the car park and took out her registers. The other glass wall looked out to the swings and play area leading to peaceful grass fields. She stood up straight and took a deep breath. It was quiet in here … for now. The empty tiered benches sat behind glass panels which formed a barrier to the six-foot drop. Stairways on either side of the seating area allowed spectators to enter from the café and walk down to a certain point, beyond which was strictly lifeguard access. Occasionally a few cocky strays would mark a territory which was never theirs in the first place, only to be rounded up and herded back into the pen.

The creak of the glass door swinging open caught their attention as one of the lifeguards, Leon, smiled his way in.

"What depth d'you want it at, ladies?" he asked with a wink.

"Zero point eight, please," they sang together.

"All the way across," Kai added.

The alarm sounded as the floor began to lower, and a few mothers and toddlers started to trickle into the viewing area.

"Look, Mum, look! Where's the water coming from?" they quizzed, pressing themselves against the glass panes, hanging their hands over the wooden rail at the top.

The pool floor slowly heaved down and water underneath came rushing over all four edges, forming a quadrilateral shoreline. Bubbles crept towards the centre like fast drumming fingertips. In the time it took the pool floor to reach 0.8 metres, Kai had gathered twenty floats, eight noodles and eight sinkers from the equipment cupboard. She picked up the folder of registers for today's classes which would finish at six-thirty, and with the two private lessons on the end, she'd be done by half-seven.

The Zoo was slowly filling up. Mothers were already descending the forbidden steps where signs clearly stated *No unauthorised personnel beyond this point.* Perhaps it could have been clearer … *Stay the fuck off poolside.* She had always welcomed mothers with little ones for their first swimming lesson and kids who felt anxious or out of sorts – but stayed away from parents whose teeth glistened with saliva.

The noise levels were rising. Hungry children crying for their afterschool snacks; younger siblings grizzling after being rudely awakened from snoozing in their pushchairs; others shouting as they ran from one end of the wooden benches to the other in a kind of zig-zag ascension, energised to be elevated at the highest level on the balcony.

A few parents were changing their kids in the viewing gallery instead of the changing rooms, their laziness exposing their naked children to predators. Knickers, socks and vests flew through the air and littered the floor. Fluffy bears and metal cars fell through the gaps at the bottom of the glass panels, and kids screamed at the thought of losing them forever. Half-eaten biscuits dropped over the edge and lay soggy on the floor.

A crescendo of mobile ringtones greeted a flustered Caren, who taught on the opposite side of the pool. She had been here for years, started as a lifeguard and qualified as a swim teacher, achieving further certification as a trainer assessor for lifeguards. She always kept Friday evenings for herself as it was "salubrious for everyone to have one night of freedom". In Kai's opinion, she was the best of the best.

Caren threw her bags down on poolside, waved in Kai's and Charlotte's direction, shook her head at the horseplay and promptly disappeared into the swim cupboard. She was putting together her own swim school in one of the private hotels nearby, and Greyton Pools with all its trappings was now just a pain in her backside.

Children were filtering down the steps, while others who had figured out the correct use of the changing rooms entered poolside through the creaky door.

Kai slides the first list of the day out of its A4 sleeve and simultaneously blows out slowly through puffed cheeks. It's Tuesday – Brother Day. The two boys stand either side of their mother's childbearing hips. She towers above them (and everyone else) with slightly stooped shoulders, and dresses older for a woman of her age. She wears round glasses, and her short brown curly hair sticks to the frames with sweat. Her mouth is tight. Her body language suggests she might say something, but Kai greets the brothers with a big hello and automatic smile, expertly avoiding eye contact with the mother. Locking eyes could provoke an attack. The older boy, Ricky, returns the hello, while young Reece recoils behind the safety of a frumpy brown cardigan, wrapping himself in the flare of an equally frumpy but lighter brown A-line skirt.

Two lane-lines click into the hooks, separating one side of the pool from the other, forming a narrow lane down the middle for Charlotte to teach her private lessons.

"Level ones, come down," Kai announces. Six children filter down, and Ricky joins them. Reece unravels himself from the brown A-line folds and follows his older brother.

Caren calls her group on the other side of the pool, and Charlotte's one-to-one is already waiting, complete with hat and goggles.

The lessons commence.

They start by sitting on the edge and splashing their feet to see who has the straightest legs, laughing as they soak the person sitting next to them. With the correct swivel entry into the pool, they walk, hop and jump from one place to the next. They blow bubbles and the ones who are brave enough make the tops of their heads disappear under the water. Except for Reece. Reece doesn't smile. He doesn't laugh and he doesn't cry. He looks at Kai, not saying a word or making a sound.

"Come on, Reece," she coaxes with a huge grin. "Can you jump up high and touch the ceiling, then disappear like magic under the water? Can you touch the floor with your fingertips?"

Reece does nothing. He watches Kai jump with her arms stretched above her head, and land with bent knees so she can touch the floor to show him. He is more complex than his brother, who takes part, enjoying himself, mixing with the other kids.

Kai notices a man standing in the creaky doorway wearing red swimming shorts. He was there last week and the week before. A tall, rounded figure in his fifties watches her and the two boys.

She tries to engage Reece but has seven other children to teach. Just one who doesn't comply makes it difficult for the rest. And with only half an hour, it's impossible to dedicate the one-to-one attention he needs. Private sessions would be better for him. When she looks again at the door, the man has disappeared.

While the others swim with their floats and noodles, Reece steps along the floor. Kai looks for anything at all that she can praise. Did he just kick both legs, feet off the floor?

"Well done, Reece," she lies. "Keep going!"

After five minutes of play, the lesson is finished.

"Great effort today, guys!" she calls. "Climb out, go and get changed and I'll see you next week." The kids rush to the warmth of their towels. As Kai is pulling out the register for her second class, a drab brown movement catches her peripheral vision, and she turns to meet the lanky figure who stands alone, this time without her boys. The brothers, Kai observes, have scuttled, wrapped in their towels, to meet the figure in red shorts who has returned from his swim, and stands again at the creaky door.

"Are the boys going to move up soon?" Her cold energy is as dark as her clothes.

"Ricky will move up," Kai replies. "Reece will stay where he is."

"We want them both to be in the same class," she snaps.

Kai internally rolls her eyes. *I suppose you want them both to fall in the* same *lake, at the* same *time, on the* same *day!*

"And you don't get on with Reece, but you're absolutely fine with Ricky. What's your problem with Reece?"

"Oh, Ricky's great! He does everything I ask, and he listens to instructions well. Reece is a little less compliant and needs one-to-one. He doesn't listen to a word I say."

"That's because you point like this." She jabs her finger through the air in an exaggerated way that makes her look like a very silly fifty-year-old trying to impersonate an American gangster.

"You need to go and speak to reception," Kai advises calmly, but her blood is boiling inside and she could erupt at any moment. She might just push this rude woman backwards into the pool. She could make it look like an accident, too. "If you don't like the way I teach" – she disguises the three ritual taps on her folder in the hopes that the third tap will send this woman as far away as possible – "take him out of my lessons. I won't be offended by that."

She makes sure this is the end of their conversation by turning her back, squeezing her shoulder blades towards one another and walking away to call her next class. She's used to this breed, and while she's sensitive to their middle-class abuse, the buoyant spirits of the children in the following lessons, along with appreciative mothers, will keep her afloat.

The rest of the evening runs smoothly. There is only one little girl, Laura, in the last group. She's tiny, about five years old, hurrying around the side of the pool because she's a few minutes late. Her green swimming hat has pushed some of the hairs down onto her forehead, and she frantically tries to force the escaping tufts back under the uncomfortable rubber cap. The Zoo cacophony has softened, and there's no one sitting on the tiered benches on this side at all. Laura looks worried as she scans the viewing gallery with wide, desperately searching eyes. He spots her first, from way over the other side of the balcony – too far away for Kai's contact lenses to make out a face. A grey T-shirt stands up, waving an arm over the heads of chatting mothers. Little Laura beams back at him, the way only a daughter does at feeling reassured she hasn't been abandoned.

As Laura is the only child who has turned up, Kai takes off her shorts and T-shirt, kicks off her flip-flops and climbs in to give one-to-one tuition. Laura will progress more in this next half hour than she would in four group sessions. Kai stands directly in front, knees bent to keep her shoulders under the water.

"Blow out your bubbles to the fishes." She demonstrates holding one float under each arm, putting her face in the water to blow out bubbles. She turns her head to the side, resting one ear on the surface. "And listen to what the fishes are saying. And then the same on the other side. Blow out your bubbles first …"

As Kai turns to rest her other ear at the top of the water, she notices a figure, half obscured by the light reflecting on the glass, sitting on this side of the viewing gallery. She commits her attention back to Laura, passing her the floats to take her turn.

"Good, Laura!" she says with a grin. "What did the fishes say?"

Laura chuckles. "Blow bubbles," she answers.

"Yes! And kick your legs at the same time." Kai completes the instruction. Laura nods eagerly, starts to kick, blow bubbles and turn her head. She is textbook.

Moving through the water, the angle of light clears on the glass to reveal the figure … a suntanned, good-looking guy she has never noticed here before. She positions herself for another look. He wears the grey T-shirt, accompanied with blue jeans and sandy Timberland boots.

From the way he's staring at her, she decides she isn't interested. He seems like a lad, probably ogling most girls … and she already has one like that.

Jason Brown.

On and off for fifteen years: emotionally unavailable, excellent at playing mind games, super non-committal and exceptional in bed. She'll probably have a raw boredom-text from him when she checks her phone after teaching.

She focuses on bringing the lesson to an end with five minutes of play. Star floats front and back, a mushroom float and picking up sinkers off the floor – oh, and a pencil jump at the end.

"That's great, Laura Bee. You've worked really hard today – you're an awesome swimmer." Laura looks pleased with herself and glances at her dad for his approval.

"OK, let's climb out, hands flat on the top." Kai talks Laura through it and does it with her at the same time. "Jump up, tummy on the side first, knee over the top, kneel and stand up." They are in sync. "You go and get changed and I'll see you next week."

Laura walks towards her dad, whose eyes sparkle with pride mixed with relief at finally being able to leave the oppressive heat.

"What d'you say?" he prompts, nodding in Kai's direction.

"Thank you." It's a timid, delicate gratitude. An endearing rare quality that always surprises and touches her heart, and a credit to the person who has taught them so.

"You're welcome." Kai means it sincerely as she stands dripping on poolside. She turns to Laura's dad who mouths a thank you.

She smiles and waves back, watching his well-built six-foot frame climb the steps and leave through the doors at the top.

The last two private lessons pass quickly, and Kai is starving. Caren and Charlotte have finished their one-to-ones and are already packing away. Kai puts her shorts and T-shirt over the top of her wet swimsuit, packs the swimming accessories back into the cupboard and gathers her bags.

"Oh, thank god that's over." Caren slumped. "How did yours go today?"

"Was OK," Kai replied. "Apart from that rude Mrs Jenkins!"

"Oh my god, I'm sooo glad I don't have to deal with her anymore. Feel sorry for you."

"Hmmm … thanks." Her gratitude was slightly twisted. "You were later today? How's it all going at Cranes Hall?" Cranes Hall was where Caren was setting up her swim school.

"Oh, don't! It's a lot of organising but getting there. Can't wait to leave this place. Oh, I meant to say, one of the swim teachers – Francis – is leaving Baker School, they're looking for someone to take her place. Are you interested? It's seasonal, cos the pool is one of those above the ground ones, in a poly-type-tunnel, so I think it's from April to about October."

"Oooh, sounds nice! Yes I *am* interested. What days?"

"Tuesdays after school and Saturday mornings. That means you give up your Tuesdays here and never have to see that Jenkins woman again … or her husband who waits at the door before he goes off to have his swim."

"I know! What's that all about?" She was glad someone else had noticed. "Anyway, yes pleeease for Baker School. I'm done here, so let's go for it – I'll do it."

"OK, I'll text you the details later. Think you'll love it. She has some clients already … I'm pretty sure you can take some from here … they'll follow you."

Charlotte ambled over to them wearily, after packing her floats and noodles away.

"How was it, ladies?"

"Glad it's over." Caren sighed.

"Did I see Mrs Jenkins having a moan?" Charlotte turned to Kai.

"Yes, you did! What gives them the right to speak to us like that? She *nearly* went for a swim herself!"

They boomed with laughter. It would only be a matter of time before one of those mothers lost their footing.

"I gotta go." Caren announced gathering her bags. "Picking up Mary and Lonnie from swim club, cooking dinner, then back in the evening for lifeguard training, walking the dogs after that, then up at six a.m. Ohhh …!" She looked at Kai over her shoulder as she scurried away, "Good luck for Saturday night!"

And that was how Caren lived her life, at two hundred miles an hour. Two daughters, two dogs, a full-on life with work, and an amazing relationship with her husband. They made a great team.

Couples like that were extraordinary.

Families like that were exquisite.

They were solid.

Kai thought of her dysfunctional "exchange" with Jason. It was hardly a relationship, but for reasons only the universe knew, after a fallout and swearing they would never see each other again, they always gravitated back towards one another.

Kai picked up her bags and walked with Charlotte to sign out at reception and say their goodbyes. She'd almost forgotten about her audition at New York New York table-dancing club on Saturday night … where you could earn "a thousand pounds a week".

Back in the car, she scrabbled inside her bag for her phone to see what delights Jason had sent her.

FANCY A SHAG?

She didn't, actually. She was tired and wanted to get home to a healthy salad and candlelit bath. She ignored him. She may have considered replying if he had written COULD I TAKE YOU TO DINNER TONIGHT? – but that wasn't his style at all.

She had met him at a nightclub. A doorman *(apparently, they aren't called "bouncers" anymore);* short mousey hair, transcendent ocean-deep-blue eyes, a fit, martial-art sturdy five-foot ten, and a very thick neck. But *bouncer* would have better described him. Bouncing his way in and out of her life, bouncing her emotions, and bouncing girls around to which day of the week suited him best.

Clearly, she was only fit for a Tuesday.

Well, she was up early to start work at the chemist for nine o'clock in the morning and wanted to get in the main bathroom for a bath tonight before her lodger.

Curly-Haired-Tony. A single guy who needed a month's stay Monday to Friday because his work as a builder had brought him down south from the Midlands. This Friday would be his last day. It worked well being a live-in landlady; new company every so often, with extra money to help with the bills. And even though guys were messier than the girls, they were a lot less hormonal.

Walking through the front door and into the living room, Kai placed her bags on the floor.

"Alright?" Tony asked. Once again he had positioned himself in the middle of the black leather L-shaped sofa, so if she sat either side, she would be next to him. "How did it go today?" He brought his feet up to rest on the cream ottoman.

"It was OK, thanks. And yours?"

"Not as exciting as yours, standing naked all day." His eyes lit up, wandering all over her body.

"Not really *exciting*," she diverted, wondering why she had ever told him. "It's the most boring job in the world."

"I'd like to have been there." She had known him for only four weeks and could have predicted his response.

Silly men.

"I'm going to have dinner, then jump in the bath. I'll say goodnight now and see you tomorrow." It was quarter past eight. She made her salad, took it upstairs and ate it in her bedroom while the bathtub filled with bubbles and lavender oil. She sprinkled in a scoopful of Epsom salts, locked the bathroom door, lit two tea-lights placed by the taps, and two church pillar candles at the opposite end in the bath corners. Through the flickering glow, she undressed and stepped into the hot soothing water, which immediately loosened her ankles. She lay back into the bubbles, placing one foot on the protruding mixer tap to keep her head from sliding under. *Bath manufacturers do not cater for the five-footers.* The pores on her chlorine-coated tightened skin began to ease with the heat and she could smell the bleach leave her body.

She closed her eyes and lay still for a minute or two, breathing in lavender; the level of the water rising and falling over her belly full of salad with each breath.

As she swapped feet on the mixer tap to release the aches of the supporting leg, she felt the day ooze away.

She was looking forward to the weekend. Friday and Saturday, she would be in the studio, and Sunday she'd be at the art market along Bayswater Road in London.

Perhaps she'd sell something this week.

And if she got her audition at the table-dancing club on Saturday night, she could leave Greyton Pools altogether.

The inside of her eyelids lit up and she flicked open her eyes. *Damn that mobile phone. Does it* have *to be in the bathroom?*

Peeling her back off the slope of the bath and feeling the cool air around her shoulders, she dabbed her hand on the towel and read the text.

YOU HAVE 5 MINUTES TO ANSWER THIS TEXT, THEN I'M MAKING OTHER PLANS.

There was a time when she would have obeyed his emotional bullying, but was used to his manipulation, craving her reaction. She didn't buckle. Switching the phone off and dropping it onto the towel, she resumed her position. She tapped the edge of the bath, firmly planting him away from her on the third tap, making sure her thighs weren't touching. Then repeated it just to be sure. Foot-free from the mixer tap this time, she slid all the way down, allowing her head to sink under the bubbles.

Chapter Two

The smell of oil paint swirled around Kai's nostrils, greeting her with the lust of Friday freedom. Wednesday at the chemist had been slow. Thursday, life-modelling had numbed all her senses, and late-afternoon swim teaching was full of the usual pandemonium, speckled with a few lovely mothers. Right now though, she was where she loved to be – surrounded by canvases, white spirit and sunshine.

She stared down at the thirty-square-inch blank canvas laid flat on the floor and wondered what on earth she was supposed to do with it. Placing one foot in front of the other, she sat cross-legged on the floor and inched her hands into a pair of clear, non-powdered surgical gloves.

She planted her left elbow to her left knee and dumped her chin firmly into her palm, fingertips curled in, gloved nails resting on her cheek. Her long dark hair was tied up on top of her head, out of the way.

She had the whole day to create … though it could easily take that long to ponder past blank-canvas-syndrome. She looked beyond the blazing white canvas, to the unread newspapers neatly spread out over the hardboard underneath. The different sized pieces of hardboard had been carefully arranged like a jigsaw puzzle, to protect the twelve-metre square off-cut lino. The lino had been rolled out to preserve the bare, wooden studio floor. Paint-proof, for sure … just in case. Twice a year, she would pull up the hardboard, take it all outside for a hard bristle brush, and lay it all down again – thankfully not in the exact same position as when she had taken it out – praise to her therapist who had been working on breaking this pattern for the last two years.

A half-hidden headline in bold large letters revealed the letters *Murd*— She couldn't see the rest of the sentence but sighed at having to neutralise the word with three taps, arranging her shoulders in the right place and positioning her already spaced-out thighs into a wider position. If she could just do it once and move on, it would be easy – but once was never enough. At least now no one in her family or anyone else would be murd … *that!*

Her eyes wandered back to the empty canvas. Starting a new one always felt tricky, but her Cobalt-Blue paint-spattered jeans, dotted with Emerald Green and pretty much every other colour in the oil-painting world, brightly reminded her that she had consistently battled through this point.

Crawling on her hands and knees to her wooden box of treasures, she opened the lid and let it rest against the wall. She peered inside as though for the first time, excitement tingling her tummy. Two-hundred-millilitre metal tubes of paint stood upright, rubbing shoulders with one another as though at a private view. The shiny new ones wore immaculate white screw caps, while older dented tubes had fashioned their own tops in the style of small dry mounds of paint, courtesy of can't-be-bothered-to-put-the-lid-back-on. Palette knives had tipped themselves into empty plastic shampoo bottles cut in half, and offcuts of wood begged to be made into frames and caressed by twelve-ounce cotton duck.

She had stopped mitring wood, joining corners and cutting the quad to sit neatly on top to lift the canvas away from the frame's edge. She had given up stretching canvas around the frames, either with a stretching tool or her bare hands, breaking most fingernails and bleeding the knuckles. She had quit stapling canvas to the backs of wooden frames and precisely folding in the corners to then prime with gesso. She never used this combined set of time-consuming skills anymore, as she had learnt over many years that it would be beaten out of the overall price of the painting by prospective buyers who understood nothing of the art process.

Glass jars of all sizes huddled together inside and outside the box. Some filled with different colours of oil paint mixed with white spirit ready to pour. Others clean and empty. A few that had housed liquid paint for so long, the white spirit had evaporated, leaving a lumpy pulp at the bottom.

Paint brushes whose bristles had hardened were kept to stir liquid paint. She smiled at the assorted mediums plus lots of other artist's collectables that she'd get round to using one day … even those Damar crystals she'd had for eight years, thirsty for turpentine to give them life as a thick varnish.

She stayed there for a few moments on her knees, gloved fingers perched on the edge of the box, not forcing the colours to come, but waiting patiently to see which ones had decided to play today. And there they were – Alizarin Crimson and Vandyke

Brown – two of her favourites that when mixed together formed a colour with no name.

Next to the standing tubes, under several tea strainers, lay an oblong tub of Liquitex modelling paste. A thick, creamy cement-like substance which added depth to any surface, thrusting artwork into another dimension. It took precedence before a single drop of paint reached the canvas. As she peeled off the lid and chose the longest-bladed palette knife, her phone silently vibrated, lighting the screen. Ignoring it, she crawled with her opened tub of modelling paste to the canvas, dipped in the knife and twirled it around, gathering the opaque off-white medium. She iced it onto the middle of the canvas in no particular pattern and with nothing in mind. It would take only a couple of hours to dry if she placed it directly in the heat of the summer sun. She positioned the canvas on the laid-out newspapers in a rectangle of sunlight formed by the window and picked up a tub of acrylic medium, Glass Beads – teeny tiny translucent beads in a white paste which reflected the light, intended for acrylics but worked just as good with oils and helped them dry quicker.

A painting never felt finished unless it was loaded with texture. A tactile finish that could be felt *physically* as well as emotionally. Using the palette knife, she scooped round the inside of the pot, scraping hundreds of miniscule beads into the bottom half of an empty Paul Mitchell shampoo bottle.

Alizarin Crimson readily oozed out of her brand-new tube, emerging like a thick worm behind a layer of glossy translucent linseed oil, and deliberately curled around to lie in the bottom of the makeshift palette. Vandyke Brown wasn't so easy today. He sported no new white screw cap – instead, he had a build-up of dried paint blocking the end. Slipping her fingers and thumb into the handle of a pair of scissors, Kai parted the blades and dug the pointed side into the top of the tube, piercing the small mound.

Wriggling it around to unclog the end, she pulled out the blade, now covered with satisfying, moist dark-brown oil paint.

She wiped clean the shank of the scissors with one of the hundreds of cut-up T-shirts she used for rags. Vandyke gave her all he had as she squeezed from one end, pinching along his metal body to the top. Even at this stage she knew he had more to give and cut him in a horizontal half, then along the edges. Peeled open, he lay almost finished, happy she'd found a way not to let himself waste. With a paintbrush, she eased the thick paint off his silvery lining and scooped around his neck, gathering the last of the bulging paint onto the wide bristles.

His carcass lay still. Gaping.

She scraped the relics of his soul into the pot, pressing the two colours gently into one another. She stirred rhythmically clockwise, timely brushing in the paste until all three ingredients were at the right consistency – too much paste would be too runny, and too little would allow the oils to take over and become too sticky.

Before her gloves got messy with paint, she checked the message on her phone.

BAKER SCHOOL – 01853 224558. TUESDAYS – 4-6PM, SATS – 9-11.30AM. I HAVEN'T GOT A PRIVATE NUMBER FOR FRANCIS, BUT IF YOU LOOK UP HER WEBSITE 'SEA TURTLES', HER DETAILS ARE ON THERE ...

Perfetto. It would mean sacrificing two and a half hours of valuable studio time on a Saturday morning, but worth the possibility at being able to leave Greyton Pools altogether. Over the years, she had slowly been whittling down six days a week of teaching. Saturdays she used to stay in the pool from eight thirty in the morning until four o'clock in the afternoon teaching one-to-ones. A never-ending conveyor belt of children streaming in one after the other. While chlorine did a remarkable job of bleaching the ends of her hair a non-negotiable ginger as a freebie balayage, she had drawn the line at her rotting toenails.

... OH AND GET RID OF THAT FUCKFACE. AFTER WHAT HAPPENED WITH YOUR EX, YOU'RE STILL LETTING GUYS TREAT YOU LIKE CRAP! XXX

Hmmm ... come down off the fence, why don't you? The incident with her ex, Luke, took place so long ago, she never spoke about it anymore. It should have broken her heart but instead had shattered it to a point just before obliteration, hanging in her chest like a splintered piece of Swarovski glass that could explode at any moment, the fractured tip puncturing the good intentions of anyone who dared to look at it. She'd then spent the following years building an impenetrable casing with an unforgiving exterior. It had learnt to beat a vastly different tune.

She looked out through the open window to the silver birch trees in her neighbour's garden, their tall tranquil trunks swaying gently in the breeze, and shimmering leaves bringing her to stillness. Eyes closed, she breathed in deeply, inhaling their spirit. As her body relaxed, she dabbed the colour-with-no-name mixed with glass-beads paste onto the canvas, taking care not to touch the modelling paste until it was dry.

She blobbed wherever the paintbrush guided, in no distinct sequence. Pushing the gooey mixture around with the synthetic bristles of the brush and laying thousands of beads next to each other. Any gaps would be filled with the next round.

When the mix came to an end, Kai stretched slowly out of her hunched position over the canvas, broadening her chest to smooth open her crumpled pecs. She slid over to the wooden box of goodies, and Red Rose and Cadmium Yellow were ready to fuse with Alizarin and the beads. They would perform a gradual blend from the velvet reds to a sunset yellow.

Swirling the paintbrush round in a jar of white spirit for a quick clean, she loaded the brush with the new colours and began to dab upwards, downwards, forwards and backwards. The modelling paste had dried, and she dabbed over that too.

Dissolving time in this realm of creation, she hadn't heard Curly-Haired-Tony walk over the garden stones to her open studio door.

"Alright?" he greeted, making her jump a little. "Thought I might catch you painting with no clothes on. It *is* my last day," he whined, his teenaged smile spoiled with an older man's wink.

"Is it that time already?" she said, standing up to face him. She tried not to smile back but was intrigued by his boldness.

"I'm gonna jump in the shower," he said. "Maybe we could have dinner together before I go? Or watch a DVD? I've got some naughty ones upstairs."

She wondered at what point over the last month she had led him to believe she could be interested in him, let alone his naughty DVDs.

"You can watch it online," she heard herself say, slightly disappointed at her participation … if there was any vagueness about him missing the point earlier, she'd just confirmed it right there. But even though Play-Away-Jay hadn't been in contact since Tuesday, she was exhausted being pulled and pinged on his elastic band of apathy. She had no energy for playing games.

Curly-Haired-Tony took a step towards her, his grin losing the pretence of playfulness. A serious hunger dipped the middle of his eyebrows, parting his full lips. After everything he had thrown at her, he'd spotted the flash of a green light.

Her laden paintbrush threatened to paint the front of his dirty T-shirt blood-orange if he came any closer. They stood like this for a moment. She didn't trust herself to say anything else but had already acquiesced to his dark green eyes with large pupils and pretty lashes.

"I'm gonna have a shower." He broke the carnal silence without moving.

"I'll get your deposit ready." She set the conversation safely back on track and was the first to turn away. Sitting on the floor and pretending to dab, she heard his steps crunching over the small stones heading back into the living room. *Where on earth* is *his deposit?*

Cleaning the brush, Kai pulled the surgical gloves over her hands, turning them inside out, and threw them in the carrier bag she used for a bin. She slipped out of her painting clothes and wriggled back into her shorts and string vest top. After wiping her hands with a rag soaked in white spirit, she went inside to wash her hands free of chemicals in the kitchen sink.

Ah yes – his deposit was in a box folder up in her room in the wardrobe. She climbed the stairs to the sound of running water from the bathroom, entered her bedroom and pulled out the pink folder that was hidden under her jumpers. Flicking it open, she picked out an envelope with the money and would count it downstairs in front of him. As she turned to leave her bedroom, Curly-Haired-Tony opened the bathroom door and stood completely naked.

Kai was desensitised to nudity, drawing nude men and women from the age of seventeen at art college. She had studied in depth all sizes of penises, vaginas and boobs. His body didn't faze her.

"Ooo." He smiled. "Are you joining me?"

"No, I am NOT! This is your deposit." She waved the envelope in the air merrily. "When you're ready, come down. I'll put the kettle on."

"Come orrn. Take your clothes orrff."

"Think you need another shower – a cold one this time!" Kai could see he was getting hard and turned to descend the stairs. "See you in a bit."

By the time he came down with his suitcase, the drinks were on the kitchen table. He leant against the doorframe slurping his tea with a defeated smile curling his lips.

"Thanks for being the best landlady," he said.

"You're welcome."

"You missed out, y'know?"

"Oh, really? On *what* exactly?"

His eyes glistened. "If I ever need to come down this way again, I'll look you up." He tipped his head back to catch the last drop of tea in his mouth.

Placing the house keys on the kitchen table, he counted his four-hundred-and-fifty-pound deposit and said goodbye. Happy to have the house to herself, she bounded up the stairs, foraged through her wardrobe and threw on a selection of sassy outfits to wear for her audition at the club.

Chapter Three

The heat of the eight o'clock July morning sun warmed Kai's skin through the windscreen, illuminating her soul with the glow of summer. She had packed the car full of paintings the night before, so she could spring out of bed at six forty-five for her third consecutive Sunday at Bayswater Road art market.

Pulling up to the kerb just after the set of traffic lights, she looked for the yellow painted numbers on the pavement that showed each person's pitch. Three hundred and seventy, it was around here somewhere. The lady who'd interviewed her at Westminster for the trader's licence had asked if she'd like the Marble Arch end or the Notting Hill end. *Did it matter?* Apparently yes. Most artists wanted the Notting Hill side or the centre of The Road to maximise passing trade. It turned out there were no spaces at the moment in "footfall-land", so she took what she was offered. It wasn't too bad, and her neighbouring artists were super friendly.

There it was. Her pitch with the upside-down numbers. The paving slab had been put back topsy-turvy after some work had been carried out. She smiled, perhaps they were abstract workmen.

She was the first of her group to arrive and, as usual, needed a wee. Stretching her arms behind the head rest and arching her back with a yawn, she watched the early risers further down The Road, hanging their artwork. They were arranging and rearranging canvas sizes and colours on the railings to fit their nine-foot-wide single pitch. Prolific artists rented two or three pitches side by side to display their artwork, which should have allowed breathing space between each piece. But the more space they had, the more they jammed in, as "It was good to show customers as much stock as you could – no point it sitting in the car!" – possibly good advice coming from artists who had been trading on The Road for fifty years "… when the shops were closed on a Sunday and people used to fill the pavement, customer after customer buying stock …" – which came as no surprise for Kai, always having a great idea for a business venture which had peaked years before. She wasn't deterred. This was only her third week, and after having patiently sat on the waiting list for seven months, she wasn't about to give up just yet.

Turning off the ignition, Kai stepped out into the summer air. It was wonderful. She looked up through one of the many plane trees that lined Bayswater Road, to see the sky twinkling behind green leaves and squirrels darting along faraway branches, winding up towards the infinite compound blues.

She waved to Clive who had three prime pitches at the entrance into Kensington Gardens. He returned her wave, a definite arc from left to right, right to left, as though drawing a rainbow with the palm of his hand.

She headed in Clive's direction for the toilets – a crummy, outdated concrete building which was an enormous disappointment for any tourist (and local) who had been tricked into believing that Hyde Park and Bayswater would glisten in the sunlight.

"Morning!" Clive bounced towards her, arms open wide, his striking powder-blue eyes beaming with each step, like they'd known each other for years.

"Buongiorno!" She returned his squeeze.

"Lovely day. It's gonna be a hot one. How'd you get on last week? Did you sell anything?"

"No, nothing. How about you?"

"Yeh, a couple of pieces. Maybe today you'll sell. The good weather brings people out."

He was right. The good weather *did* bring people out … to sit in the park and enjoy the sunshine, while artists stood under the cool shade of the fabulous trees, selling their souls.

"Hope so." Her optimism was genuine. "Happy selling."

Turning left through the gate and under the trees, the view of the Italian Gardens slowed her footsteps. She paused for a moment, inhaling deeply to absorb the shimmering light on the water fountains and the hazy shades of green that faded far into the middle distance – a familiar feeling of belonging. She sighed, declining nature's offer to play with the realms of time and listen to the sounds of the world – and promised that she would, one day.

She entered the stone outbuilding that passed for toilets. At least the cleaner came early on a Sunday morning, allowing the first wee of the day to be quite a pleasant experience. It would look (and smell) quite different in there by three o'clock this afternoon.

Stepping out once again under the trees, she focused on the trading side of the railings. More artists had started to arrive, giving Bayswater Road its Sunday identity and lifting her heart. Wading back through the dazzle of Clive's gaze, she noticed his neighbour's canvases lining the railings. Copies of Frida Kahlo. Pretty good they were too.

She stood for a moment and caught herself wondering if he'd sold anything last week. Turning around, she locked eyes with the copy painter, who had emerged from the boot of his car, fingertips curled around opposite sides of an exact copy of *Roots* – Frida's poignant dream of giving birth. He lowered his painting to get a proper look at her, and she found herself swimming in another pair of blue eyes – greeny-blue this time, more of a French Ultramarine, accentuated with a dark rim running the circumference of the iris. They had a watery sparkle, alive with mischief.

"Hello," he greeted her politely. "Haven't seen you here before. Are you new? I'm Chris, by the way."

"Hey," she smiled. "Yes, started three weeks ago I trade a bit further up. I'm Kai."

"Oh, OK. Have you sold anything yet?" That seemed to be the general point of interest. "What number's your pitch?" He fired another question, his canvas now lowered all the way down, one corner resting on his trainer for protection.

"Three seventy. No, I haven't sold anything yet. How about you?"

"No, it's been weeks since I sold anything. I've been here for ten years, and it's getting worse every year. I might come up and have a look at your work in a bit."

Saying goodbye, she moved on before hearing any more doom and gloom about Bayswater Road having had its day.

She walked back up the pavement, and more artists were filling the gaps: Plastering Pete, with big mustardy red and yellow abstracts sculpted on board; Seascape Sarah, who brightened the rails with turquoise seas; Figurative Phil, who presented a mixture of nudes and abstracts inspired by his love of the piano and the female form. There were a few others that jumped pitch every now and then to see if the change in location would help sales – though it didn't seem to make any difference.

She carefully took her paintings out of the car one by one and leant them against the side door, still in their bubble wrap.

Her pitch was a metre and a half high of brick wall, and just over a metre more of railings were set on top of that. She lifted two big canvases onto the wall, pulling the bottom edges out and tipping the top edges back to rest securely at an angle. Grabbing hold of the railings, she hopped up to stand on the ledge.

The world was fascinating at this level. Closer to the boughs of the trees, floating away from the grey fumes, a more peaceful perspective. Eyes closed, she tipped her face towards the sun, allowing the rays to seep into the pores of her skin and warm her bones. Problems faded away up here.

Shuffling along to the first of her paintings, she picked off the bubble wrap, watched it waft down to the ground and hooked the string at the back over three Georgian-style finials. Balancing was a little trickier now, but she'd found a system; turning her body to face the rails square on and hanging her heels off the edge of the wall, she could manoeuvre around the front of the paintings along the ridge. It was a faff. At least it hadn't rained yet. She'd had metal rods made up, bent at a sloping angle, to fit on to the finials and had bought tarpaulin to drape over the rods and clamp with clips. But she hoped she'd never have to bother. In other words, it was never going to rain on a Sunday in London.

She jumped down to straighten her paintings, pausing at one in particular which had pulled her into its mystery. Abstract painting was a magical process. Once the cerebral chatter of how a painting should start and finish was annihilated (usually by ignoring the harsh criticism of realists who love to tell you that their six-year-old could have done a better job), the mind becomes still. And when the mind is quiet, enchanting creations flood through the portal.

She was so absorbed with how Zinc White had merged with Alizarin Crimson, giving a misty pinkish cloud, that she hadn't noticed the guy standing next to her.

"Beautiful," he said. "How much for all three?"

She half jumped, turning to meet the Middle Eastern accent. About five-foot seven, a full head of black hair, a goatee, dark shiny eyes and a businesslike smile. He was referring to three canvases she had arranged in a row, two purply ones on the outside and a blue one in the middle. She hadn't thought they'd sell as a trio, and they definitely didn't work as a triptych. She tried to quickly add each individual price up in her head … which was useless, seeing as she'd failed maths twice at school, despite her disappointed, persistent father who was not going to let her leave secondary education without it. Her eyes were frantically working out an invisible sum on the bushes behind the rails – *five plus five is ten carry the one, nine plus nine is ...* the numbers broke free from their columns, spiralled and overlapped each other in a foggy maths-muddle, and spun away. It was somewhere around three hundred pounds.

"Three hundred and fifty pounds," she said, smiling back at him.

"Are they oils?" he asked, stepping closer to the canvases for a micro inspection.

"They're oils and mixed media." She stood back, giving him space to feel their energy, remaining silent so as not to disturb his connection. He didn't seem the type to need coaxing, and she didn't like doing that anyway. She didn't want to coerce people into buying her artwork. She wanted them to buy it because when they stood in front of it they were brought to an inner stillness, transcending the colours and composition, to a place that they couldn't quite remember.

He took a step backwards and to the right, adjusting his viewpoint. *There.* He'd found it, surrendering to the silence as he tried to remember. After a few moments, he faced her.

"I'll give you two hundred and fifty. Cash. But I don't have the money on me now, it's at my hotel. I'm staying at the Millennium Hotel in Knightsbridge. Do you know it? This is my number." He took out a black leather wallet, slid out his card and held it out to her between his index and middle finger. "You can call me if you get lost. What time do you finish here?" he asked, extending his hand.

"Around seven o'clock." She felt obliged to shake it. The conversation had suddenly picked up speed, and she found herself being swept along. What just happened? She'd agreed to a sale without a deposit and was now the delivery service as well! She guessed he wouldn't have done that in Selfridges, or anywhere else for that matter, but even on her third week, she was beginning to notice a certain impiety towards the artists along The Road.

"I'll see you just after seven. You can wrap them up, so you don't sell them," he called over his shoulder, his businesslike smile now turning a little derogatory.

She thought about that. No. She wouldn't wrap them up yet. Instead, she folded a long piece of bubble wrap, laid it on the concrete ledge, unhooked the three pieces and carefully positioned them in a row, leaning the top edge against the rails. She wanted more people to see them first, and anyway, she may not find his hotel, or he could change his mind.

Isandro pulled up in his car behind hers, while Seascape-Sarah and her husband Jim were still unpacking the blues and hues.

"Morning," she greeted them all at the same time.

"Good morning." A stereo of voices spilled out of the cars. It was a special feeling, being with other artists in the sunshine.

Pleased with herself for a sort-of-sale, she opened the passenger car door, sat on the front seat as most artists did, and waited to spot a group of people ambling towards her. Then she would step out of the car to stand casually by her pitch, available for any questions from the public.

Any at all.

About anything.

And the usual question was "Where is the entrance to Hyde Park?"

She watched mothers with toddlers, teenagers and couples. A diverse rising crescendo of syllables, fading into the hum of car engines. She stood up and walked to her pitch. Crowds of people passed on by.

No one stopped. Perhaps she'd had her only sale of the day. An early morning sale. *Is it really this difficult to sell artwork?*

"Good morning," the familiar Argentinian voice greeted her. She gave Isandro a hug. His hugs were stiff and awkward, but he managed it. "How's it going?"

"It's going good. I sold these three – I think." She grouped the three paintings sitting on the bubble wrap together with an airy sweep of her hand.

"You *think*?" he asked, raising an eyebrow.

"Well, he hasn't paid for them yet. I'm taking them to his hotel later."

He raised the other eyebrow. "Ah, that's great! Did he leave a deposit?" Oh dear. She felt silly enough as it was.

"Errrrm … no, he didn't."

He made no effort to hide the customary Bayswater they-all-say-that, you-should-have-taken-a-deposit look on his face, though he did try to disguise his lack of faith that this guy would even be at the hotel (if indeed it was the right hotel). "Well, that's OK, see what happens later."

Kai felt herself shrinking but managed a nod as Isandro turned to set up his pitch.

Seascape Sarah greeted her with a hug. Her husband, Jim, came over too.

"Sold anything yet?" he asked with the glint of kindness in his eyes that some older people seem to have.

"Well, yes, I have. These three, dropping them off to him later at his hotel."

"Oh, I say!" Sarah joked. "A sale is a sale. Well done."

Kai didn't dare mention he hadn't paid for them yet.

"It's gonna be a nice day." Sarah shifted the conversation. "Let's hope we all sell today."

"Hope so. Have you been painting this week?"

"I've got a new one. I'll show you when Jim's got them all out of the car."

Jim was dutifully emptying their car of paintings, cased in neatly homemade bubble wrap bags. They completed a very healthy duo which had worked well for them for many years.

"Great." Kai let them set up, knowing what it felt like when you've just arrived and want to get the work out to show as many people as possible. She liked Sarah's work, the ripples of the ocean, and how she'd captured the wet sand as the tide pulls away. Moving to Clacton had inspired fresh brush strokes from her balcony, looking beyond the waves.

The street was getting busier, and the railings that ran along the edge of Hyde Park were growing colourful and bright. Through the gaps between the advancing shoulders, she spotted a full head of black hair, a cheeky smile and the same bluey-green eyes that she'd encountered earlier. The copy painter was walking towards her, grinning like a naughty child. She smiled back at him.

"Alright?" he said when he was beside her. He looked at the railings, not sure which canvases belonged to whom. Isandro's were on the left, Seascape Sarah's were on the right. "Are these yours?" he asked, spot on with his centre choice.

"Yes, from the big square blue and white one on the right, to the big blue, green and white on the left." He didn't look impressed, but she wasn't trying to sell to him, so it didn't matter. She expected his reaction; he hadn't found his own style, perhaps copy artists never did. They were exceptionally gifted painters but couldn't allow their artistic hand to fly free.

"Have you sold anything?"

"Yeah, those three on the bubble wrap, in the middle."

"Oh wow!" His delight seemed genuine. "That's pretty good going, selling on your third week. It takes ages for people to sell up here. When's he coming to get them?"

Oh crumbs! People want to know every detail.

"Er … he's not – I'm dropping them round to him at his hotel in Knightsbridge later." She waited for a disparaging comment, though it didn't come.

"Oh, that's great! Do you know where you're going? I've dropped paintings off to clients before … do you know London?"

"Not really. But Knightsbridge is that way, down that road, right?"

"Yeh, all the way down to the bottom and …" He wriggled his phone out of his pocket. "What's the hotel address? We can look on Google Maps." He bent his head and tapped his phone. His profile exaggerated his long dark lashes complementing his light eyes, and his slim lips uncovered sharp teeth with pointed top incisors when he smiled.

"So, this is that road there …" He tilted the phone towards her, moving closer, inviting her to share the view on his screen. She leant in to look at the map but wasn't really concentrating. "At the end of that road, turn left then right, and the hotel should be along here somewhere." He enlarged the map with his finger and thumb. The Millennium Hotel was depicted with the red upside-down teardrop with a dot in the middle. It looked so easy on this tiny map, but she knew the hustle of London traffic and lack of right turns would complicate things.

"Oh right, OK, that's great, thanks." She made herself sound more confident with directions than she'd care to admit. "I'll find it." Of that, she was sure. She had made a sale, and she was going to collect her money … even if it took her until midnight.

Chris walked over to the three canvases to take a closer look at her technique.

"Are they acrylics?" He lightly smoothed his fingers over one of the canvases.

"No, oils."

"Are they?" he retorted, like he almost disbelieved her. "How do you do that with oils?" It was a question she loved to hear. Most people who asked that question knew it was a skill. Usually, most comments were "I can do that" or "It looks like a child did that!" but realistically, they wouldn't know where to start (or stop) and had no idea of how ludicrous they sounded. "You've definitely got your own style. How d'you do it?" he repeated. She wondered whether to tell him, though often found that other painters would interpret the technique in their own vision, formulating a completely different result.

"I squeeze some paint into a jar, mix it with either turps or white spirit – depending how luxurious I'm feeling – shake it up, leave it for a few hours or a day, strain it out into another jar so it's smooth and pour it on. Then manipulate the canvas, e voila! Do that with a few colours at the same time, so they fuse with each other, and you can pour more on when and where you need it." She kept the glass beads technique to herself.

He frowned. "But how do you control it?"

"You can blow the paint to a certain point or use a hairdryer, and it blooms into the colours next to it. You can tip the canvas too. Sometimes you lose a lovely formation in the middle while trying to cover the edges, so it's better to mix all the colours at once and try to do it all in one go." She'd just exposed her secrets but could see by the smirk on his face that he had never ventured away from copy painting or realism in his life.

Three young lads dressed in shorts and trainers, slightly unsteady on their feet from summer beer, teetered past and nearly knocked into them. Chris steered Kai out of their way.

"Look at the price!" exclaimed one of the lads, his white T-shirt neatly hanging out of his back pocket while his hand waved half a bottle of Peroni in the air.

"I know, right." Kai played along. "It should be much more!"

The boys looked confused and stumbled away.

"Did you go to uni?" Chris asked. "Or are you self-taught?" It was a fully loaded question, but she was prepared for it. You didn't persevere as an abstract painter without the condescension of egotistical twits.

"Yeah, I went to Southampton Uni."

"Oh right. Did they teach you about perspective, and did you do any life-drawing?"

It was her turn to smirk. "Of course. Most abstract painters have the discipline of drawing, but we choose to specialise in how something feels, rather than how it looks."

It was clear she wasn't convincing him, and she wasn't bothered. He had no clue, and that was OK. Perhaps he'd find his own artist's voice one day.

"Do you know these people next to you?" he asked.

"Yes, that's Sarah" – she pointed – "and Isandro. Have you not stretched this far before?"

"Not really, we don't tend to move away from our pitches down there."

She found that odd. Ten years of exhibiting and he didn't know anyone more than three or four pitches either side of him.

"I know who people are." He guessed her thoughts. "But haven't really spoken to them much." He nodded to Sarah as he said it, and she nodded back. It was a we-don't-really-know-each-other-but-I've-seen-you-up-here-for-years-so-will-acknowledge-you type of nod.

He turned his attention back to Kai. "So what else do you do?"

"Oh, a few things. I teach swimming, do a bit of life-modelling for an art college and work in a chemist. I have an exhibition running at a local theatre that's on for another couple of weeks."

"Oh, a swimming instructor," he said, ignoring the exhibition. "Perhaps you could give me a few pointers. I'd like to improve front crawl, though I get so out of breath. That's probably how you stay so fit. So, when do you find time to paint?" She didn't like that question at all. It meant that she wasn't a full-time painter … but how were you supposed to be a full-time painter with bills to pay when you couldn't sell any artwork? It didn't make any sense.

"Most people find the breathing hardest to get right. They tend to go a little too fast instead of pacing themselves. It's just practice and slowing it down a little. I paint at the weekends and will give up working at the chemist soon. How about you? Do you work anywhere else, or do you make enough money selling paintings?"

"I have a commission for five grand that I'm working on at the moment. It's taking me forever; I just haven't got the motivation to finish it."

"Oh wow! A commission. What's it of? How big is it?"

"It's about seven foot by three foot. Long and narrow. A biblical scene, as the lady is quite religious."

"Oh. Not surprised you lost your motivation," she said with a grin.

He laughed as he took his leave. His five-foot-six, compact physique walked away, hands loosely in his trouser pockets, elbows casually flowing back and forth with his steps. He did "the nod" to a few artists along the way as he melded into the crowds. Kai sat down on the front seat of her Astra, in the warmth of the mottled sunshine, pulled out Julia Cameron's *The Artist's Way*, and randomly opened it at a beautiful quote by Joseph Chilton Pearce: "To live a creative life, we must lose our fear of being wrong." Oooh, she loved this. It was powerful and liberating. Perhaps she could print it out in humungous letters and hang it between her abstracts. She zoned out of the bustle of the non-buying public and read her book in that broken sort of way, when trying to keep a look out for any sales.

She couldn't focus. Instead, her mind replayed the reels of her audition last night.

*

She had asked a taxi driver at Ealing train station for directions on foot to the club, and he'd seemed pleased that she wasn't taking his cab for such a short distance. His directions were precise, and she'd found herself at the entrance of the club, under blue neon letters – *NY NY.* A pink neon cocktail glass with a stirrer to the right and an outline of a woman's bare foot in an invisible stiletto was lit in neon purple to the left. A tall, imposing doorman stood at the top of a descending staircase, ready to start his shift.

"Hi," she said. "I'm here to see Lilly."

"Down the stairs and to the left," his deep West African accent guided. "Follow the stage round and she'll be in the dressing rooms." He hadn't seemed impressed with her jeans and trainers, but she had outfits in her small rucksack.

She'd almost skipped down the stairs, into the dim glitzy lighting below. The bar twinkled with empty hanging glasses, and a dark-haired barmaid was flirting with another doorman. *Good luck with that!*

Kai turned left as instructed, passing the raised stage in the centre, a shiny pole at one end and two at the other. Girls who were dressed and ready to work sat on red velvet tub chairs at small round tables. Four comfy armchairs lined up in a row were separated by gold fishnet curtains for private dances. She walked up a wide step lit with round tiny white bulbs to the elevated level, where more red tub chairs were set around tables, and sections of gold see-through curtains housed more armchairs.

It was empty on this side of the club.

She approached a black wall, the top of which disappeared into the shadows. It looked like a dead end. Slowing her footsteps and wondering where to go, Kai spotted a dark hazy staircase. She stood at the top and peered down to the mists below, then followed the plum-red carpeted steps, edged with a black strip, to the bottom.

She pushed open a black door labelled *Changing Rooms* and walked in.

Mirrors reflected topless girls applying their heavy make-up; others in their underwear were choosing sparkly dresses and blingy jewellery. Huge bulbs lined the edges of the mirrors, lighting the otherwise dark basement.

A tall slim African girl wrapped in a small pink towel stepped out of the only shower, her wet skin glistening with droplets of water. She smiled a row of straight, white stunning teeth, her hair wrapped up in a towel, toenails painted Hooker Red.

There were lockers with wooden doors, though not enough for every girl. A pleasant soft aroma filled the air, a comforting smell she couldn't quite make out.

Sitting on a chair in a small alcove was a woman of about sixty-five with brown, shoulder-length wavy hair and dark-brown eyeliner. She smiled at Kai. Not a warm smile – nor a cold one. Just I-am-the-boss. Clearly this was Lilly.

Kai didn't even need to audition. She'd been asked to take her clothes off, and they'd chatted for about twenty minutes through bare nipples and buttocks. Lilly's voice, cracked from too many cigarettes, explained the setup. The stage names of the dancers would be called from a list – so make sure you knew who was before you. If you were giving a private dance at the same time you were supposed to be on stage, the next dancer on the list would take your place. Choose two favourite songs, an upbeat first, and a slower second, and let the DJ know. On stage, keep your dress on to the first track, and strip down to bra and G-string for the second – guys wouldn't want a private dance if they saw too much on stage. No touching the clients, and the clients were not allowed to touch the girls. Ten pounds a dance. The extended area acted as an overflow for when the main part of the club was full. Girls paid the club thirty pounds at the end of every evening.

She could start the following Friday.

*

A rumbling tummy and sleepy eyes told Kai she could do with moving around and getting something to eat. The time on her mobile phone read quarter to four. She could pop to the small sandwich shop on the corner by that curious passageway for a cheese and tomato toastie on brown bread and a green tea. Closing Julia Cameron, taking her handbag and locking the car, she walked to where Seascape-Sarah and Jim sat on their front seats.

"Hey," she said. "How you getting on?"

"Oh, alright." Sarah smiled, looking up from her newspaper. "Spoken to a couple of people, but no serious buyers."

"It's still early, you may get that sale as you're packing away like last week." Two ladies had been walking past Sarah just as Jim was placing a painting inside a bubble wrap bag. One of the ladies was holding a white Yorkshire terrier, and she noticed a dog on the shoreline in one of the paintings. The dog wasn't quite the same as her own, but she loved the painting and bought it.

Sarah laughed. "Oh, wouldn't that be nice!"

Crossing the road at The Swan pub, and turning the corner into Lancaster Gate, she passed the Corus Hotel and walked to the end of the street. Brook Mews North lay to her right – a small avenue that led the eye into its mystical dimension. On her first week at Bayswater, when she had come to find Helen's Café, she had paused on this very spot. The Mews had turned her head several times, offering familiar perspectives that she couldn't quite remember: an energy of another time.

She climbed the concrete steps to the coffee shop. Thankfully, there was no queue – a fabulous result of not eating lunch at the same time as everyone else.

"Hi, Kaiii." The lady behind the counter greeted her with a magical Thai accent that would make anyone who had been to Thailand close their eyes and wish they were back there.

"Hey, Helen." She briefly wondered if that was the lady's real name. "How are you today?"

"I'm good! Have you sold any paintings?"

Kai nodded. "Yes, sold a few this morning." She left out the details as she ordered her toastie and handed over a ten-pound note. She really must get organised and make a salad for her Sunday lunches – cheaper and healthier. "Thanks, Helen, have a great week, see you next Sunday."

Resisting the crisps and chocolate, Kai headed back to her pitch, stopping at the corner of the street. The scene gave a very different feel from this covert side of The Road – as though standing in the wings on a stage, watching a show in which she played a part. There were no smiles on the backs of the traders, and their desperate heavy shoulders carried the repetitious runaway load of "Are you here next week?" or "We're going to get something to eat, we'll come back later" or "Where's the nearest cashpoint?"

Pete tried harder, carefully lifting one of his plastered artworks off the rails so the couple he was talking to could see it away from the distraction of other paintings either side. It was a good trick, encouraging prospective buyers to come a little closer, running their fingers along the surface to feel the texture, weight and quality of the frame. Yes, perhaps a little more interaction with the genuinely interested public would bring them one step closer to visualising the artwork in their home.

The couple thanked Pete before walking away empty-handed.

Checking for traffic to cross the road, Kai's attention was caught by huge abstracts to her right. Splashes of colour brightened large canvases, as bold brush strokes played together, forming incomplete circles and roads to nowhere. Bursts of vertical yellow expressions crossed diagonal blues, while greens and oranges sprayed the deep reds underneath. Drips of purple and white had been dribbled from a height in Pollock style. She looked for the artist but couldn't see anyone.

At six o'clock in the early evening sunshine, a few artists began to pack away. She may as well do the same. There were no more sales happening up this end though she *had* spotted one or two people pass by with a rectangle of bubble wrap tucked under one arm. And *that* was the cruel trick of Bayswater … one person in two hundred would stroll by, teasing all the artists, giving them a sliver of hope that a buyer could come along at any moment and do the same to them. That's why a handful of artists stayed here until nine p.m. during the summer … just in case.

Sensing the demise of sales for the day, Kai opened the car boot and laid the three sold paintings in the boot so she could package them neatly with bubble wrap and masking tape. This was the worst part of the day: packing it all away to take home again … and why on earth did the canvases never seem to stack the same way they had in the morning?

She said goodbye to her neighbours and headed off to find The Millennium Hotel in Knightsbridge, slightly anxious at not finding anything at all in London rush hour. "Just follow this road, all the way into Knightsbridge, turn left at the bottom, then right, and it should be along that road somewhere." It was easy for *him* to say. He didn't have a map phobia brought on by family summer holiday adventures in the motorhome with a very irate father who couldn't understand why shouting didn't make it any easier for his two teenage daughters to read road maps.

Noticing her phone battery was low as she waited at the traffic lights, she decided to save as much of it as she could for an urgent use of Google Maps. The lights turned green. She moved with the cars, heading down West Carriage Drive. So far so good – horse track on the left, car park and pathway to the Serpentine, driving over the bridge now and heading for Knightsbridge.

She reached the end of the road and turned left as the map had showed. *Oh golly! Now where?* She wasn't familiar with any of these roads but relaxed into the heat, windows open – the slow traffic allowing her to look out for Imperial College. She couldn't see it. Had she driven past it? Or was it over there? Oh, it couldn't be that one, no right turn. *Oh, it probably IS that one, damn – passed it now!* Perhaps she should turn around … no U-turn. She turned left and pulled up to the kerb to let the car behind her pass. A fairly quiet road that only just allowed a three-point turn. She headed back to the junction – *No Right Turn! Seriously?* She turned left, back to where she was headed along the main road, probably still in the wrong direction.

She pulled over to give the man a call. It was the first time she'd looked at his card properly. Gold letters on a black background read *Zakariya Amlani Real Estate.* The contact details were underneath. Nothing fancy. Plain and simple.

"Hello?"

She recognised his accent.

"Hi, it's Kai. I'm trying to find you. I'm not quite sure where I am, though I'm on my way." She glanced at the orange digital numbers on the clock in the centre console of the car. Three minutes past eight? Wow! Nothing like getting lost in London to while away an hour.

"Look, it's OK," he said. "If you can't find it, we can leave it."

She almost exploded but composed herself.

"No, it's fine," she said firmly. "I'll be with you soon." She honestly wanted him to have them. They were beautiful pieces of work. She ended the call, drove to the end of the road and could only turn left. It was a wide road and strangely peaceful for London. She pulled up by a huge white building to decide what to do. There was no one around to ask for directions. Perhaps it was time for Google Maps. She placed both hands on the top of the steering wheel and leant forward to rest her chin on her knuckles. A group of people circling out of a revolving door snapped her attention. Above them in big silver letters read *Millennium Hotel.* She thanked the universe, picked up the phone and hoped what was left of the battery would survive the call.

"I'm outside. I found it."

"Ahhh, great. I'll come down."

As her phone sang its last beep of the day, Kai wearily stepped out on to the road. It had been a long day, and she was tired. She opened the boot and placed the canvases on the pavement, leaning them against the wheel arch as he walked towards her smiling with a wad of rolled up notes in his hand.

"I'm sorry that you had trouble finding me." He handed her the money. "Count it," he advised.

"Ah, it's OK, got here in the end. Thanks," she said as she counted the cash. "Your paintings …" She handed them to him one by one. He looked as though he may struggle to carry all three. "I could give you a hand?" she offered. "Not sure if I can leave the car here though."

He looked at her, his shiny black eyes widening. "You know, if you want to come up and give me a massage, I can pay you another fifty pounds."

She thought about this. She was drained and needed to freshen up. Even though she could shower in his en suite and her takings for the day would rise to three hundred pounds (possibly more if she kept her clothes off), she declined.

"Oh thanks, but I'm gonna head home."

Suddenly, he could manage all three paintings and looked embarrassed for asking.

"Great, and thanks again," he said. "I love these paintings. You know we don't really like people in paintings, we like abstract."

"Enjoy them." She smiled, knowing he would. Climbing back into the driver seat, she waved him goodbye, and drove to the end of the road, not really having a clue where she was, and looked for signs for the A40.

Pulling up to a set of traffic lights at an enormous junction, she wondered at her parallel universe; at this point, she'd probably just be finishing the massage and going on to whatever else. *How much would he have been willing to pay?* And could they have left out the kissing? It was only sex after all, and if he had taken her from behind, she wouldn't have had to look at him. Sex took on a new meaning when you were single … and broke.

An hour and a half later, she was nearly home. She yawned as she turned into her road. Her bed was calling her. She'd unpack the car tomorrow. Parking in her space at the side of the house, she noticed Jason's vehicle parked in the lay-by across the road. He jumped down from his van before she had turned off the ignition and marched towards her.

Chapter Four

"I suppose you think you're being clever, ignoring me!" he raged.

"I'm going to bed. I've been at work all day and I'm tired."

In the half-light from the street lamps, she could see his clenched jaw and tense shoulders. If she opened her front door, he would push his way in. If she didn't, he would probably kick it down. This was going to be tricky.

"Shall we talk about this tomorrow?" She tried to reason with him. He grabbed her shoulders, slamming her back against the brick wall.

"Let me come in." He lowered his face to hers. "I'm not going anywhere until I come in and we talk."

"You seem a bit too angry to talk tonight."

"You fucking make me angry!"

"Keep your voice down!" She was aware of her neighbours and how late it was.

"I don't care who hears me," he growled. And it was true. A couple of months ago, he drove round to her house at ten o'clock at night with her vibrator, smashed it to bits on her doorstep with a hammer, and sent a text on his way home stating the obvious – that if she didn't want to see him anymore and use it with him, she wouldn't be using it with anyone else either!

"I *said* let me *in!*" His hot breath spittled in her face, and he emphasised the words with two more thumps of her shoulder blades into the bricks.

She knew his games, but this was the first time he'd gotten physical. She was marginally confused but his blustering bulk didn't scare her. Frustration swept through her veins. It was impossible to move sixteen stone of muscle on her own. The only way to defuse this situation was to let him in.

"OK." She surrendered, too tired to argue. She unlocked the front door, and he followed her inside.

In the hallway, she kicked off her trainers.

In the living room, she pulled the beaded metal chain to pivot the vertical blinds closed.

She sat on her favourite side of the leather sofa, the only end that had an armrest. Jason sat on the open end of the L-shape. Sliding open the drawer of the side table and taking out a box of long matches, Kai lit the bergamot and lavender scented candle.

"Why haven't you answered my texts?" he demanded.

"I've been busy." She swung her legs up onto the sofa and tucked her ankles into the cheek of her bottom. *And you're a* cock *who has no respect.* "What's the matter, Jay? Doesn't anyone want to play with you tonight?"

"You're the only one for me." His eyes shimmered in the candlelight, his face serious. Anyone who didn't know him would have believed him. Crumbs, he actually believed himself! If she didn't melt every time she saw him, she would have ended this for good a long time ago.

"And don't turn this around." He leant forward, his square jaw and chiselled cheekbones fluttered the butterflies in her tummy.

"You only text me when you have nothing else to do," she said. "Or rather, no *one* else to do. Anyway, it doesn't matter. I've been working and painting for Bayswater."

He had clearly forgotten she'd been in London all day.

"Did you sell anything?" He softened a little.

"I did. Three canvases."

"That's good." They were short, awkward sentences.

They sat in silence, Kai too weary to open up a deep dialogue, and Jason too receptively defunct.

"I'm going to make a hot chocolate," she said. "Do you want anything?" she asked, knowing full well that he didn't drink hot drinks.

"No thanks. I've got some water in the van." He stayed on the sofa while she went into the kitchen, switched on the under-cupboard lighting and made her drink. Tucking the oat milk carton neatly back into the fridge, she pushed the door closed with her hip and wrapped her hands around her mug. A stiff soreness was creeping around her upper back. Clearly there wasn't much to say to each other, but she knew how the evening would unfold. She took a deep breath and shuffled into the hallway.

"I'm going upstairs for a shower," she called from the doorway. "You can stay or go, it's up to you. If you're coming up, could you bring the candle, please?"

He followed her up the dusky-pink carpeted staircase, put the candle on the bookshelf and placed his phone face-down on the bedside table. He always did that. Lying back on the pillows, he unzipped his jeans and peeled them off. He never wore underwear.

Kai placed her hot chocolate on her bedside table and switched on the Himalayan salt lamp. "I won't be long," she said. "I'm up early tomorrow, have to unload the car before work."

"It's OK, I'll be gone before you get up."

He always did *that* too. God forbid he should stay past six o'clock in the morning, let alone help her! She showered in the en suite, lathering the foam shower gel over her body a second time and washing all the suds away, patting the froth down the plughole with her toes. When she walked into the bedroom, Jason was unsurprisingly completely naked.

Rolling deodorant under her arms and smoothing moisturiser over her face, she lay on top of the covers next to him, but not touching.

"Nightie nightoh." She kissed his cheek, knowing that neither of them were going to sleep.

"Just need the loo," he said. While he was in the bathroom, his phone lit up the side table in a muted screen-down way. She didn't really want to … but did it anyway. Turning the phone around, she read the name on the locked screen in bold letters.

MARIA.

Goodness knows how many girls' names he had in his phone. If there weren't a billion girls with the name Maria, she may have shuddered at the name of her sister.

Chapter Five

When the alarm softly played a gentle melody at seven-thirty, Jason had already left. There was no sign of him having been there at all. He was like a phantom lover. Last night had played out exactly as predicted. She had suppressed any urges to ask about the text from the mysterious Maria. He had climbed back into bed spooning behind her and kissing her neck; both feeling aroused, they had made lust, which was always astounding – especially after a tiff – and he had vanished before she awoke.

She tapped the phone screen to turn off the alarm – no time for snoozing this morning. She chucked off the duvet, brushed her teeth, showered, got dressed and grabbed her car keys. She carefully unloaded each painting, stacking them in their bubble wrap along the wall in the log cabin studio. Half an hour later, she mixed one banana with chopped up celery together with a scoopful of plant protein and a teaspoon of spirulina powder in the blender and drank her breakfast. At eight-thirty, she set off for the chemist ready to start work at nine o'clock sharp.

Since her new night job was to start on Friday, there was absolutely no point working at the chemist anymore. The owner, Farrukh, accepted her resignation, and they agreed on two weeks' notice. It had been a very pleasant eight months working with this family-run pharmacy, and in that funny kind of way, she would miss them. But at least she now knew that Nurofen was essentially the same as Cuprofen and cost more than double the price, arnica was good for bruises, magnesium paste brought splinters to the surface of the skin, and if you run a slide film roll through the wrong setting on the photo machine erasing all the crucial photos from a one-off business trip, you get one dangerously quiet businessman who has a reel of over-exposed negatives and no slides to present to his team.

She definitely wasn't going to make her millions as a famous painter by hoovering up the chemist floor or sporting throbbing muscles for a life-drawing class. *Think bigger* – that's what the hundreds of self-help books sat on her bookshelf howled at her. This Friday would be her biggest thinking to date.

Her phone vibrated.

THANKS FOR LAST NIGHT. I FEEL CLOSER NOW WE'VE MADE LOVE. WHEN CAN I SEE YOU? XXXX

Guys really are *that dumb!* It was all about the sex. And why was he using the words "made love"? He had never made love to her. But perhaps, in Jason's world, this was how he loved her. She eased up a little and wondered why she was allowing him to love her this way. Paradoxically, there was a certain safety in this non-committal co-dependency. It was possible that this was the only tune they could dance together in this lifetime. She imagined that all the other girls he simultaneously treated this way felt as exasperated as she did. Each one attempting to tame the untameable.

HEY. GLAD YOU'RE FEELING BETTER. I HAVE A BIT TO DO THIS WEEK, SO I'LL KEEP YOU POSTED. I KNOW THURSDAYS YOU'RE USUALLY WITH THE GUYS, BUT THAT'S ALL I HAVE FREE? X

She wanted to keep every evening free this week for her usual exercise classes at the gym, ready for Friday. If he really wanted to see her, he could sacrifice his training regime for one night.

THURSDAY'S GOOD. WE CAN GET SOMETHING TO EAT. I'LL GET TO YOURS ABOUT EIGHT. XXXX

He hardly ever invited Kai round to his house. He used the excuse that it was always a mess because of four understandably grumpy dogs who hardly ever got walked. Also, the cat was getting old and would have a wee anywhere she pleased, and downstairs smelt of sweaty guys who descended on a Thursday to make full use of his training quarters. He had converted virtually the whole of downstairs into a gym so the lads could practise ju-jitsu, taekwondo and any other style of beating the hell out of one another.

Eight o'clock meant half past. She knew him well enough to add half an hour to whatever time they agreed. On this occasion his tardiness would suit her, as she could get a half-an-hour swim in after work.

After lining up all the paracetamol boxes and stacking as many Benylin for Chesty Coughs as she could fit on the shelf, she vacuumed the shop floor, said goodbye to Farrukh and headed to the local gym to start her pump class at seven o'clock. She preferred not to train where she taught; crumbs, it would always feel like she was at work … which reminded her – she needed to give Francis at Sea Turtles a call.

It was turning out to be resignation week. Francis had already handed her notice in at Baker School, leaving in a couple of weeks. Kai could gently inform selected parents at Greyton Pools that she would be leaving and if they wanted to book their children in, to let her know as soon as possible. That meant she'd only be giving two weeks' notice, but she was pleased about that … what had Greyton Pools ever done for her? Always backing the customer and never supporting their staff.

At home that night, she typed up her name and phone number ready to hand out to a selected number of parents tomorrow, popped them in her swimming folder and flopped into bed.

Chapter Six

"You told him to hold his breath to get to the other side. I don't understand why you're not teaching him to breathe. *I* used to teach swimming."

Ohh hurrah! A parent who was a swimming teacher ... can it get any better than this?

"As a swimming teacher yourself, you will understand, then, that the problem with following the ASA levels is that they don't teach the correct breathing until level three. We would all love to encourage the breathing as each individual is ready, but ..." Kai takes out a piece of paper with all the tasks that needed to be completed before a child can move up and hands it to the mother. "One of the requirements to move to level three is to complete five metres without putting their feet on the floor. When Damon lifts his head to breathe, he puts his feet down. I cannot move him up unless he completes the five metres. He manages to get all the way across in one breath, which means he can move up to level three where we focus on the correct breathing. You said you wanted him to move up because he is nine years old in the same class as six-year-olds."

"Yes, he's embarrassed of being the oldest and the tallest in the group."

"Then let's get him swimming five metres with his face in the water because he can do that easily in one breath and move him up so we can focus on the correct breathing."

"But I don't understand why you're not teaching him to breathe."

Is she for real?

"Because when the next instructor sees he cannot complete five metres without standing up, he or she will move him back down again. He either stays in level two with the much younger kids for another term because you want him to breathe properly, or he moves up and learns the breathing in the next level where the children are more his age. That way, he is out of level two." *Most parents would be grateful that their child is moving up; now please use your brain and book him in to level three or teach him yourself.*

"OK," the mother dismisses rudely. Thankfully, Kai isn't inviting her to Baker School. Shame really, because Damon is no problem at all.

The brothers haven't turned up today – maybe the mother has taken Kai's advice and moved them to another group. At the end of each lesson, Kai speaks to chosen parents and discreetly hands out her details.

Before the last group lesson is about to begin, Joe from reception walks round poolside in his blue overshoes, motioning for Kai's attention.

"Just to give you a heads-up." He leans close to her ear. "There's a mother complaining that her child has nightmares about her swimming lessons." He tilts his head to the side. "Mrs Morone?"

"Oh, Tilly's mum." Kai makes the connection. Joe nods. "Tilly always seems so happy in class; it's as though the parents have more of a problem than the kids!"

Joe smiles, nodding in agreement. On his way out he stops by Caren, bends his head in the same way and mutters something in her ear too. She throws her hands up in the air with exasperation and glares up at The Zoo. *Perhaps parents should be banned from watching their kids' swimming lessons.*

Little Laura isn't lucky enough to have a one-to-one again this week and walks round the side of the pool with the others in her group, Tilly included. They start the lesson as usual, hopping, skipping and jumping. Heads under the water and making a splash. The lesson runs smoothly, and this week Kai feels Tilly's mum's eyes bore into her back as well as Laura's dad's ... but for a very different reason. At the end of the session when it's time for play and picking up rings off the floor, Tilly can't quite manage to get deep enough to grab her ring.

"Good try, Tilly." Kai is conscious of saying one word out of place. "Try again. Let's stand close to the ring first, touch it with your toes, stand straight like a pencil – hands at the tops of your legs, jump up, and as you land, bend your knees on to the floor, disappear under the water, slide your hands down – pick up the ring."

Tilly tries again but can't seem to grab the ring with her fingers.

"Give it another go, Tilly. You're really close."

Kai notices a movement to her left on poolside. Tilly's mum has ignored all the signs and squeezes into a small gap behind Kai and the wall, brusquely marching her way towards reception. Kai continues with her lesson, jumping up high and landing with bent knees, sliding her fingers down her thighs to demonstrate how to pick up the ring.

"If you're feeling like a deep-sea diver … you can dive down head first to pick up the ring. Spot the ring so you know where it is; maybe you can see it through the top of the water or feel it with your foot. Or … you can have a sneaky look with your magic goggles under the water. Take a jump, throw your head down past your knees." Kai bends in half at the waist, head down to her knees. "Bottom up to the ceiling, straighten your legs like you're doing a handstand and kick your legs."

The braver kids give it a go; some get stuck halfway because they haven't stretched out their legs to a vertical position. They pop up and try again. Kai demonstrates, changing position, talking them through it step by step.

"Spot the ring first, so you know where it is. Dive your head down …" Kai doesn't see Tilly's mum trying to pass to get back up to The Zoo. "Bottoms up." Kai bends down. Tilly's mum has crept up behind her and is too close. Kai's bottom knocks Mrs Morone towards the edge of the pool, her foot slipping over the drop. Mrs Morone topples for a moment. Kai stands up and tries to catch the woman's flailing hand but misses; it seems Tilly's mum is poised in slow motion before losing balance, falling backwards into the pool. Clutching her handbag, a look of clumsy confusion torments her face. She cascades into the clear blue depths; water splashes high as she back-flops, the light fragmenting her body as she sinks.

There are gasps from The Zoo, and mutterings. *Is someone laughing?* Kai gathers her group to the side of the pool and sits them on the edge. Mrs Morone's feet find the pool floor as she rights herself.

"I'm soo sorry!"

Kai is genuine, *but you know full well you shouldn't be on poolside.* The lifeguard moves quickly to the edge and offers Mrs Morone his hand to heave her out of the pool. She waves it away coarsely and hauls herself out. Her clothes are heavy with pouring water. Her fair hair, now darkened by the wetness, sticks flat to her head, and black running mascara joins the tracks of washed-out eyeliner. Her face is scarlet with rage or embarrassment – it's hard to tell.

"I'll get you a towel." The lifeguard has lost the sense of urgency.

"Come on, Tilly!" Mrs Morone growls, ordering her daughter to leave the class, and squelches after the lifeguard. She does not say a word to Kai or look in her direction.

"Two hands on one side, roll over onto your tummies and slide back in." Kai composes herself and continues with a distracted class, half of whom enjoyed the entertainment, the other half perplexed as to why a fully clothed adult had joined their lesson briefly.

At the end of the session, Kai hands out her details to the select few.

"She deserved that." Laura's dad sniggers as he looks down at the piece of paper. "Oooh, what's this?"

"I'm leaving soon, setting up my own swim school. But keep it quiet for now."

"Oh no!" He seems genuinely disappointed. "Though great for you. OK, will give you a call to book her in." He wraps Laura in her towel and walks her towards the changing rooms.

Two private sessions later, she has finished for the day.

"Oh my god!" Caren can't stop laughing. "That was hilarious! Did you push her?"

"No, I did not!" Kai chuckles. "I'd like to take the credit, but it was truly unintentional."

"She's sooo stupid. Probably made another complaint. But good! – you can do without parents like that."

"Serves her right!" Charlotte joins in. "She won't walk around poolside anymore."

As the three of them sign out at reception, Joe informs them that Mrs Morone has now booked Tilly in for private lessons with Charlotte … who rolls her eyes to the heavens for all the help she can get.

"All yours!" Kai relishes.

Back in the car, Kai checks her phone for any messages.

Sorry, can't make Thursday. Xxx

Chapter Seven

Kai parked the car in a side street, a five-minute walk from the club. The same doorman was at the top of the stairs, busy with his mobile phone. They murmured hellos and she bounced down into the music below.

A few of the girls were already dressed, sitting in the tub chairs, having a drink. She recognised a handful from her interview last Saturday. Walking past the stage and heading for the changing rooms, she descended the dark staircase and opened the door at the bottom.

The familiar scene of half-naked girls, mirrors and lights greeted her, along with the soft scent that reminded her of something she couldn't quite remember. She felt at ease.

She chose an unoccupied stool, sat down in front of a lighted mirror, opened her holdall and pulled out her make-up bag. She laughed to herself. She hated make-up. Never wore it. Hadn't worn it since she was fourteen when she overdid the eyeshadow in Shimmering Pink, darkening the corners with Knight Divine Grey, and thickly lined her lower eyelid in black. Sometimes she'd underline the black eyeliner with a jade green. She'd put blusher on her cheeks the way a six-year-old paints her mummy's face (a bit like she was doing now) and had never had a clue what to do with foundation, so steered clear of it. But she *did* remember how to wear mascara, coating her long lashes and taking them up to her eyebrows in a thick black luscious realm of infinity. She applied the goo – and couldn't wait to take it off.

"Hi." The girl next to her used her own mirror to acknowledge Kai in hers. "I'm Diamond." Oh crumbs! She hadn't thought of a stage name. She wanted to keep Kai. She looked back at the girl, noticing her smooth, moisturised, shiny dark skin. She sat in black matching underwear, straightening her hair.

"Oh hi, I'm Kai. I haven't got a stage name yet … do we need one?"

"No, not really. Kai's nice. It's kinda different for a girl." She had an obscure accent – American, perhaps. She turned to look at Kai in person. "My real name is Aniyah." She stood up, picked the straps of a red dress off the hanger, holding them wide at the top while she carefully stepped into it. She wriggled it up her perfect body, slipping her arms in and adjusting her boobs. She was stunning. She elegantly placed her feet into plastic heels and said she'd see her upstairs. Oh, and remember to check the DJ's list of girls so she knew when she'd be on stage.

Kai unzipped her sports bag and took out her underwear from Ann Summers. A sexy black G-string with a red bow on the front, paired with a black see-through bra with matching bow. Sitting back down on the stool, she sprayed her neck, forearms and backs of the knees with Deep Red by Hugo Boss. She pulled out her long purple velvet evening dress with a split all the way to the top of her right thigh. Easing her slim body into the soft material, she found the black suede high heels with an open toe at the bottom of her bag. They were the only pair of high heels her feet allowed her to walk in, let alone do a couple of sexy dances on stage. *Whatever happened to trainers and hot pants?*

DJ Paul was friendly with good energy. On discovering that they both listened to Smooth FM, she renamed him DJ Smooth and gave him her two songs: "Staying Alive" by the Bee Gees for the first tune, and Madonna's "Justify My Love" for the slow, seductive second. Kai searched his list for her name. It was about halfway down, under Lola. Who on earth was Lola? DJ Smooth pointed to a girl in a sparkly green dress, with long dark-brown curly hair. She looked back at his list to see Lola's choice of songs: "Lazy" by X-Press 2 and "We Belong Together" by Mariah Carey. Good – these would be her cue.

A group of girls had formed a circle in a quiet corner of the club near one end of the bar. They sat chatting, drinks on tables.

Kai didn't need to be part of the gang. Instead, she sat on a red tub chair by herself not too far away and scanned the club. Before any girl could approach a guy, she had to wait until he had bought himself a drink at the bar or was served his drink by a waitress and had sat down at a table. Then they would pounce – boobs first.

Fridays and Saturdays were supposed to be the busiest nights of the week. After twenty minutes of sitting with her back straight and one leg crossed over the other, she wondered what time customers would start filing in.

It was half-past nine … and more of a trickle than a file.

Smart shoes, jeans and trousers descended the stairs, each step revealing more of the person. Shirts and T-shirts came into view. Finally faces accompanied bodies, and male vibration was on the radar. Young men, bald men, old men, good-looking men, large men, skinny men, shy men, cocky men, arrogant men, married men, single men.

She could see why the girls chose this corner to warm themselves up for the evening. It appeared that they were having a drink, but their clever minds were taking bets on *who* had the largest wallet, *who* would be the easiest to convince that any of these girls could possibly have an interest in them, and *who* would be so drunk that they couldn't decipher a twenty-pound note from a ten-pound note.

The official presence of men in the building flared the extravaganza as DJ Smooth announced the first dancer, Sydney. Her first song was "Uptown Funk". Sydney elegantly climbed the three steps to the stage, her long fair hair flowing around her shoulders. She shuffled to the single pole in tempo, took hold of it with one hand, and performed the outside step into a pirouette, her silver sequined dress twinkling as she twirled around. She wasn't super skinny, and she wasn't overweight – somewhere in the middle, a healthy lass. Not toned, but not wobbly either. She *also* wore the plastic slip-on heels.

Guys sat and watched. More men were stepping down the stairs, to the beat of Mark Ronson. Some sat at tables, others ordered drinks. Girls had started to ease out of their lairs to prowl towards the nightly income. Kai wriggled her hips to a middle-aged man who sat alone drinking a beer.

"Hi," she greeted him. "Can I sit with you?"

"Of course." He pointed to a chair beside him. She relaxed into it and crossed her legs, the split in her dress revealing bare skin to the top of her thigh.

"That's a beautiful dress. What's your name?"

"Kai. And you?" She leant in closer, placing her ear near his mouth – not to tease him, but because she couldn't hear a darn word he was saying. She would make a useless barmaid.

"Rob."

A girl in a white dress came marching round the curved end of the stage and stopped in front of them both, resting her hand on her waist.

"D'you wan' a dance?" she barked above the music. Kai was slightly confused. Was this girl offering her a dance? She was about to ask what she meant but was saved the muddle.

"There's a guy over there who wants you to dance for 'im," the girl continued. Kai glanced over to where two guys sat on the other side of the stage, then turned her head slowly back to Rude-Blonde.

"I'm having a chat at the moment." She nodded to Rob who had noticed the awkwardness. He wondered what was going on, and why this girl had come to take Kai away from him when he was just warming up to see her naked. "I'll be over in a minute."

The girl left. "I'm sorry about that." Kai watched him sip his beer and shake his head slightly as if to say "no worries at all". She waited a couple of seconds for him to ask her for a dance, but by the time he had taken to swallow his drink and say anything at all, Kai thought it best to bank a definite dance from the guy on the other side of the club.

"It was nice to meet you. I have a dance waiting," she said, standing up and pushing the tub chair behind her with the backs of her knees. He nodded, looking slightly defeated. She felt a little bad, but she had thirty pounds to pay the club tonight, and a guaranteed dance was better than chitchat. It wouldn't be long before he was lost in someone else's nipples.

Kai wandered in her black stilettoes towards the guy who had requested her presence. He had even pulled a chair out for her. She smiled and sat down comfortably. Mark Ronson had stopped playing and on stage, Sydney was writhing out of her silver sparkly dress to INXS's "Need You Tonight", kicking it to one side with her plastic-heeled foot.

"Hi," he said. "I'm Vincent."

"Hi, Vincent, I'm Kai."

"I'm here with my friend, Steve." He indicated the guy sitting beside him, who looked a lot like Penfold from Danger Mouse. He was cheerfully chatting to Rude-Blonde, and waved a hello, knowing that his voice couldn't compete with one hundred decibels of Michael Hutchence.

"It's my birthday today, so we're celebrating."

"Ohhh, happy birthday."

"I bought myself a new jeep. Not sure how safe it is round here. I parked it on the road, just outside the front. D'you think it'll be alright?"

"Well, I don't really know. I heard someone saying it can get a bit rowdy from people coming out of the club next door." She wasn't lying. The night club next door was called Sunrisers, and a couple of the girls had said it could get quite fractious after hours. Vincent's face dropped its smile as he looked past

Kai, his glazed eyes widening as his imagination wrecked his new jeep.

"Oh! Maybe I should go out and move it."

"Hmmm … it's up to you. I parked in one of the side streets."

"Oh, I'll risk it," he concluded. "D'you want a drink?"

"I'll have a water, please. I don't drink anymore."

"Oh?" He seemed surprised. "Any reason why?"

"Yes, it was a calorie *thang* in the beginning. And I like to be in control of the evening. If I don't like where I am, I can leave and go home for a hot chocolate and a warm bed without having to wait for a taxi or rely on friends … and also a few embarrassing moments that I won't go into, but let's just say alcohol doesn't suit me."

"Alcohol doesn't suit *most* people." He laughed. "Hold on." He called the waitress over. "Still or sparkling?" he asked Kai.

"Still, please."

The waitress slipped off and returned with one small, clear bottle on her tray and placed it on the round table.

"Do you work in the day?" Vincent asked, as Sydney's second dance came to an end and another girl with short fair hair wearing high cut, glitzy white hot pants, literally got down on her hands and knees and crawled up the three steps to the stage.

"Yes, I'm an artist, an abstract painter. I also teach swimming and have just handed my notice in at a chemist where I used to work."

"Oh wow!" He seemed impressed. "How do you sell your artwork?"

"I have a website – though don't really get many sales from it. I've just got a pitch along Bayswater Road near Hyde Park;

sold a few last Sunday, and I have an exhibition running at the moment in a theatre in Raselberry."

"Oh right, yep, I know where that is. I live just around the corner from there, Capes Village. Have you heard of it?" She *had* heard of it. She used to pass through it with her ex, Luke.

"Yes, I know it. So, what do *you* do?" She diverted the conversation not only from her ex, but also from her lack of sales.

"I'm CEO of a company called Prelude. We design and sell the latest ergonomic equipment to offices for people with a physical need."

"Oh, that's really cool." They both turned to watch The Crawler on stage, lying on her back, opening her legs wide, then closing them together again. She tucked her thumbs into the top of her hot pants, lifted her hips for a reverse curl, eased the hot pants over her very tight bottom and rolled them up her thighs. She paused here for a moment, dropping her heels to her butt cheeks, then back up towards the lights that disappeared into the dark depths of the ceiling. The next time her heels were down, she took hold of her hot pants, slid them around her knees all the way down past her shins, peeled them over her heeled plastic shoes and threw them off the stage. *More plastic heels!*

"Here's my card." Vincent rummaged in his wallet. "The surname's Kane – it means 'battler' in Irish. My family's from Ireland, but it's a long, complicated story." He waved his memoirs away with his business card before handing it to her. She quickly looked at it out of courtesy before tucking it away in her small handbag.

The Crawler, now on her knees, stepped one foot forward, stood upright, picked up speed and headed towards the single pole. Arms stretched high above her head, she jumped off the floor, landing only her two hands on the pole, and sailed her body round clockwise, in a kind of floating kneeling spiral. Kai had no idea how she did that but was looking forward to her turn.

"Whereabouts is your pitch on Bayswater?"

"I'm number three hundred and seventy, near Lancaster Gate tube station. I'll be there this Sunday."

"I might come and see you one Sunday."

"Oooh, I'll look out for you."

The Crawler finished her two tracks, and several girls, one after the other, teased guys from the stage through their sexy routines. Some made eye contact while rubbing their bodies, others blew kisses as a way to hold men's attention, so that when they finished dancing they would head straight over and chat them up. A girl in a sparkly green dress was heading towards the limelight, quickening her steps. Kai just caught the end of DJ Smooth's announcement, "… the lovely, LOLAAAA!"

"Oh, I'm next, after her." She nodded to an already up-side-down body clinging to the pole and a dress that covered Lola's face, leaving only her long brown hair hanging out the bottom. The club had a full view of her matching black bra with G-string and a healthy set of abdominals.

"Oh, OK, so come back after that, and we can carry on chatting."

"For sure." *More chatting!* Kai wondered if this was going to be as difficult as making an art sale. "She's got another song to do first." Kai turned and noticed Penfold, sitting on one of the red armchairs behind the gold see-through curtains, with Rude-Blonde leaning her chest over his face, dangling her boobs a centimetre from his nose. He was mesmerised, smiling like a child opening a Christmas present and finding the toy he'd always wanted. Rude-Blonde rippled her body to Mariah Carey.

"He likes blondes," Vincent said almost in disgust. "There's one who works on Fridays, but she doesn't seem to be here tonight. She's quite nice actually, but blondes don't do it for me …" He nodded in Rude-Blonde's direction. "That one tried chatting with me but that's when I sent her over to you." He laughed.

"Yesss, she didn't seem too happy about that!"

Lola teardropped down the pole to finish on the last beat of Mariah, and sauntered off the stage. DJ Smooth thanked her over the mic before introducing Kai.

"Oooh, that's me – I'll be back in a moment." She picked up her bag.

"Yep, go and do your thing. You can leave that here; I'll look after it for when you come back." She trusted him. There was nothing in it anyway, apart from a "Casting Couch" lipstick and his business card.

The deep grooves from the first few bars of "Staying Alive" hit the speakers and reverberated around the whole club. Most of the girls were too young to have heard of the Bee Gees, but their ears pricked up anyway, and guys jiggled in their seats.

"Oh yeeaahh!" A man half stood up, punched the air and clapped his hands. Kai wiggled up the steps, the bass pounding in her chest. She sang the words out loud and felt a deep connection with the lyrics. Tonight, she revelled that her life was going nowhere but didn't need anyone to come and help her – this was *her* gig. She twirled in her heels, edging closer to the single pole, took hold with one hand and slinked her way around. She didn't know any of the moves and made them up as she skulked to the music. She giggled to herself, enjoying every second. Every now and then she went to the end of the stage where Vincent sat completely transfixed, to undulate.

As the Gibb brothers faded out, Madonna slowed the tempo, which was ideal as Kai's last spin landed her neatly to her knees on the floor with the pole between her thighs.

She sang the first line to the flashing lights above, deciding that there was no one in the club that she wanted to kiss in Paris. There was also no one's hand she wanted to hold in Rome, but she *did* want to run naked in the rainstorm (on her own), so she aimed this one at Vincent who smiled, nodding his head to the beat. She lifted her buttocks off her heels, kneeling high as she slid her hands up her ribs to slip one of the dress straps off her shoulder, leaving it to dangle around her upper arm. She took hold of the pole with one hand, rippled her body up to standing, and after one complete cycle of twirls, stopped to face Vincent. Her spine rested against the metal, hips gyrating whilst she peeled the other dress strap all the way down past her elbow and lifted her hand out of the loop. Half of her black see-through bra poked out of the top, and she slinked the other arm out of the dangling strap, rolling the dress down to her waist. She snaked around like this a little longer, then turned her back to Vincent, looking over her shoulder at him to keep him engrossed.

As Madonna whispered *wanting...waiting...*, Kai tucked her thumbs into the scrunched-up material around her waist and began to slowly pull her dress down over her bottom, folding forward from the hips, hauling herself back up in time to turn and face Vincent, miming the words *to justify my love.* Not that she wanted anyone to justify her love, but she was getting into her role … and he seemed to like it. She carefully stepped out of her dress and headed back to the pole. She wasn't sure about turning upside down yet. The last time she did that was on the climbing frame at junior school … and while the stage was a softer landing than the primary concrete playground, she didn't think she could make collapsing on her head in a crumpled heap look like part of the routine.

Through the flashing red and white lights tinged with green and blue, she placed her hands on the pole one above the other. Gathering momentum, she swung her knees up to hug the pole and spun round in what she later learnt was called the Fireman Spin.

It was beyond fun. An escape from people's obedience to society's archaic ideas of how to earn a living.

As Madonna faded away, Kai found she had finished on her knees by her dress. Taking it in her hands, she stood up, walked down the three steps, climbed back into the straps, and wriggled it up over her boobs, arms in place. She straightened it before walking back to her empty chair next to Vincent.

"Very good, very good." He clapped as she sat down.

"Thank youuu."

"You obviously enjoy that. When this next song finishes, would you like to give me a dance?" he asked, feeling a little bolder after a couple of drinks.

"Of course, let's go in there." She pointed to an empty red chair behind the gold net drapes. He stood up and Kai led the way. He sat on the chair, legs open, inviting her to stand between them.

Her first private dance. She carefully slid into the space between his burgundy crocodile cowboy boots and started to sway her body, tilting forwards here and there, having absolutely no idea at which point she should start undressing. Not too soon. Then again, he had just seen her on stage and wanted to see more of her – no, *all* of her – in the next three minutes. Thirty seconds into Rui Da Silva's "Touch Me", she slowly slid her arms out of the straps and pushed her dress all the way to the floor, kicking it out of the way. She let him watch her for a few seconds before turning her back to him, reaching her arms behind to unhook her bra. Holding her hands over the cups and peeling her arms out, she turned to face him. She teased him for a moment before placing one hand then the other inside the cups to let the bra fall, draping unintentionally around his thigh. She wondered if she should move it, but decided the bra added the touch she wasn't allowed to give.

She circled her breasts around under her hands, finally revealing her nipples. She bent forwards placing both hands on the cushioned leather behind his head and set her nipples a millimetre away from his mouth. He sat like an obedient dog, waiting for his treats. She stood up straight to slide her thumbs into her knicker elastic, pulling one side down then the other, in a kind of winding motion, revealing nothing but bare hips. He shifted in his seat, sitting up, hungry for her to take them off. Kai turned away from him, and slowly bent forwards, taking her knickers halfway down her thighs. From this inverted position, she could see him between her legs and reached her hand through her thighs to stroke her bottom. Standing up, she covered her waxed Hollywood with one hand, leaving her knickers around her thighs, and continued to gyrate. Finally, she placed her legs closer together, pushed the knickers down to her shoes, stepping out of the holes praying they wouldn't get stuck on the buckles, and slowly released her hand to reveal all.

Vincent's enormous grin tipped his head to one side, unable to tear his eyes away from the mound between her smooth bikini line. She placed her hands on the chair either side of his head, rippling her naked body. *It would be much easier to actually sit on his jean-covered genitals and not have to balance in these preposterous heels,* but this wasn't a lap-dancing club. *No touching, remember?*

As Rui Da Silva's last beats danced their way into 50 Cent's "In Da Club", Kai wondered where her rolled up, twisted pair of knickers had ended up – far beneath Vincent's chair possibly. She crouched down to have a look, but he casually waved his hand.

"Aww, let's have another one," he announced with an embarrassed schoolboy look on his face. Pleased that she didn't have to scrabble about on the floor just yet, she swayed to the next song.

"Of course." She smiled. It was much of the same scenario, just easier as she didn't have to take clothes off. The freedom of being naked: no nonsense, plain and simple.

When the song finished, Vincent reached into his back pocket for his wallet. He pulled out a couple of notes, trying to decipher in the dark whether they were tens or twenties.

"Is that right?" he asked.

Kai checked, holding the notes close to her eyes and angling them towards the brighter light of the stage. *No, it's not right.* A ten-pound note and a twenty – ten pounds too much ... *but it would pay the house fee tonight.* She wondered whether to tell him, aware that her faltering would give her away.

“Yes, that’s right.” She reluctantly took advantage of his tipsy impaired vision. She found her knickers, picked up her bra which had dangled over his thigh and put them on while he watched. She stepped into her dress and led the way out of the curtain back to the chairs where they sat and chatted some more. She had lost track of time and wondered whether she should circle the club to find the rest of the night’s wages. Vincent sensed he may lose her.

“Come on,” he encouraged confidently. “Let’s have another one.” He led the way this time, walking past their first chair as this was now occupied by Rob, the guy she had walked away from earlier, enjoying the body of the African girl she saw step out of the shower on the night she came for her audition. Vincent found a chair two spaces along, sat down, spread his legs and encouraged Kai to do her thing … which she did – much better this time. Not so wobbly in her heels and keeping sight of where her clothes landed. When the song came to an end, he asked her for another dance and another. She kept her clothes off, dancing solidly for the next hour, truly working for her money. She had no idea of the time and didn’t need to know.

At the end of the last dance, Vincent claimed he had spent his quota for the evening. She wasn’t really counting but had placed every ten-pound note he had given her after each dance into her handbag. She dressed again and he followed her out to the red velvet tub chairs.

“Let’s have another drink.” He motioned for the waitress to come over. “You must be thirsty.” She now understood the need for that shower downstairs. Perhaps she’d bring a small towel next time or the purple lightweight swimmers’ chamois that one of the parents from Greyton Pools had bought her last year for a Christmas present.

"You're not driving home, are you?" she questioned, sounding like the drink-drive police.

"No, we'll get a cab." The care of his new jeep seemed forgotten in alcohol. He nodded to where Penfold sat, two girls slinking over him. "Steve spends about four hundred pounds every time he comes. He has a favourite blonde – only works on a Friday, though she's not here tonight," he repeated.

"Doesn't look like he's too bothered by that." Kai laughed. Men were easy to please. Show them a bit of flesh, crack a rude joke or talk about sex, and their brains nearly fell out the end of their cocks.

The night was coming to an end. DJ Smooth announced the last dance on stage, and half of the men had already left.

"Well, nice to have met you." Kai said her farewells to Vincent, leaning over and planting a kiss on his cheek before standing up.

"You too. I might see you at Bayswater."

She smiled, not really caring whether she saw him again or not. Pleased with her night's work, she turned away, waving goodbye to Penfold through naked ribs, who managed a wave, glasses askew. Downstairs in the chatter of the changing rooms, girls were counting their money.

"You cleaned up tonight." Diamond grinned, sparkling with genuine delight.

"Yeh, did alright, thanks – was good." Kai's sports bag was where she left it, and she began to undress. Kicking off her heels, she could smell the scent that she couldn't quite place and saw girls wiping their faces, shoulders, armpits and under their boobs with … baby wipes! *Of course,* the soothing scent of being cared for.

Kai counted her money – two hundred pounds, pretty good for her first night. It wasn't quite the thousands that others had talked about, but it would pay the council tax this month, or her contact lenses, or new oil paints and materials, or petrol, or food. She sighed at how easily money could evaporate. She started the drive home wondering if it was possible to have what you wanted in life. Did she even know what she wanted? Perhaps it wasn't about getting what you wanted … it was *the getting* of what you wanted (and possibly never got!). She gasped, her eyes widening … *an eternal getting. Oh crumbs!* She slid her hands together at the top of the steering wheel, hunching forwards to slump her chin to her knuckles. She planted two blinks close together and the third further away on the passing trees. Then did it again. And again...

Chapter Eight

"He seemed really interested," the lady at the theatre told Kai. "He came in on Sunday and stood looking at it for ages. Think you may have a sale."

"Oooh, that's good!" Kai wondered who it could be, then thought of Vincent from Saturday night saying he lived not far from Capes Village. "What did he look like?"

The lady thought it an odd question and described the man's appearance to fit Vincent's. *Oh no!* Kai didn't want him to feel obligated. *And oh, doubly no* ... Kai's mind zoomed from A to Z in the way that her therapist was always reminding her to watch out for ... she hoped that didn't mean *she* was obligated to *him!*

"I really do think he'll buy it." The receptionist misread the look of worry on her face. "Said it was for his bedroom, to go above his headboard."

At seven hundred pounds, it was the biggest, most expensive piece in the exhibition. Sweeping shades of reds across a six-foot by five-foot canvas lured the viewer over a volcanic surface of oil and mixed media.

"Ummm? Oh er … yes, I'm sure he will, that's great! Well, keep me posted – see you soon."

It was her Tuesday off from life-modelling, and she'd booked a session with her therapist. On her way, she stopped at home to check on her latest piece in the studio. This canvas was nearly finished, just a blending of the glowing reds and yellows to finalise. Although you couldn't see them now, in six months when varnished, the hidden deeper colours would magically appear.

Her phone silently vibrated. She took it out from the back pocket of her jeans.

THERE IS A MASON DO THIS SATURDAY NIGHT FOR THE GUYS UP IN LONDON. I COULD TRY AND GET TO YOU AFTER THAT? IT WILL BE ABOUT HALF ELEVEN?

Ahhh, a booty visit, how divine! She decided not to validate Jason's philandering behaviour.

HEY! I'M UP EARLY ON SUNDAY FOR BAYSWATER. MAYBE A NIGHT NEXT WEEK?

There was no reply, and she didn't expect one. He could go to his silly Mason do and get up to whatever it was they got up to there, which was sworn to secrecy. Men really did think women were daft!

Taking her swimming bag for work, she headed to her therapist, wondering what to talk about today. When it seemed there was nothing more to say, a topic would pop out of nowhere and one hour could pass like seconds. Parking the car, she walked down the narrow alley between the terrace houses to the back garden gate and rang the bell.

"Hello, Kai." Jane invited her into the purpose-built extension at the back of the house for private clients. It was Kai's favourite space. Jane was late fifties and wore round glasses to fit her warm, friendly face.

They sat down opposite one another, Kai's chair next to a table with a box of tissues that she'd only ever used once. Jane extended both arms outward, inviting Kai to open the session.

"Well, I don't really know what to talk about today. Oh, I might have sold a painting … to a guy I met at the table-dancing club, Vincent. Oh, the club … went well, earned two hundred pounds dancing for him. Was a lot of fun, men are sooo silly, they turn out the cash for seeing naked bodies!"

Jane nodded, smiling. "So you enjoyed it. That's great! And a possible sale too?"

"Well, yes, I think so. But if it's the guy at the club, it kind of feels that it's not legitimate."

"What do you mean?"

"Well, it feels like I had to take my clothes off for him to buy it. And if he *does* buy it, then I may feel like I owe him something." Kai looked out the window to her favourite Scots pine tree in a neighbouring garden a few doors down and blinked the three ritual taps on a branch.

"It's his decision whether he wants to buy it or not," Jane said. "When you buy clothes from a shop, the shop assistants don't feel like they owe you something. They have an item to sell, and it's the customer's choice to buy it or not. He bought the painting because he liked it; you didn't earn the sale by taking your clothes off."

"Yes, that's true, but why can't someone just buy a painting because when they see it they fall in love with it – like the guy at Bayswater."

Jane raised an eyebrow.

"Oh, I haven't seen you since then – gosh, it's been a while. Yesss, sold three paintings at Bayswater the other Sunday."

"This is great! You're a successful artist. And you didn't have to take your clothes off for him," she added.

"I know. If I could sell like that every week, I'd be happy. Well, he *did* ask me if I wanted to give him a massage in his hotel room when I dropped the paintings off. I almost thought I owed him one for buying the paintings!"

Both of Jane's eyebrows went up this time.

"I refused – think a sexy massage is worth more than fifty quid. I mean, if men are prepared to part with their cash so easily, it has to be worth my while?"

Jane, professional as always, showed neither approval nor disapproval. She continued to listen, matching Kai's enthusiasm in parts and mirroring her sadness in others.

"Anyway, if I can earn two hundred pounds a night, I can afford to leave Greyton Pools. Oh … my bottom knocked one of the moaning parents into the pool last week. It was soo funny. I didn't do it on purpose, but it was hilarious."

Kai continued to relay her events of several weeks to Jane's moving eyebrows, smiles and timely giggles. As the session drew to a close and they said goodbye, Kai paused at the door and turned to Jane. "Oh – and I think Jason is seeing my sister, but we can talk about that next time."

Chapter Nine

"How did it go on Saturday night?" Kai asked Jason while walking his two huskies across the fields from his house.

"Oh, it was OK, just the usual boring guys. I *told* you that when I spoke to you on the way home." He seemed preoccupied, looking at his phone, then stuffing it back into the side pocket on his shorts. "I'm sorry I couldn't make Thursday the other week, but it *is* training night and …"

"Oh, it's OK, I know. I was busy that week and wondered if you could have changed it around, but it doesn't matter."

The dogs walked in front on extendable leads, their noses consumed with every blade of grass.

"How was the club? Can you pay off the mortgage now?" he asked.

"It was OK, made two hundred pounds."

"That's not bad. You could probably earn more at Stringfellows in London."

"Probably, but one thing at a time. I haven't actually left the chemist yet, or Greyton. Need to get the swim school up and running first."

"If you do it properly" – he ignored the swim school – "you could make a couple of grand a week, like my friend Natasha."

Oh, of course – like your friend Natasha – *whoever* she *is! And what do you mean "do it properly"? I* am *doing it properly!*

They walked round the corner to the cul-de-sac where his house sat at number four. A misty, grey-blue Ford Focus was parked on the road outside his house, half blocking the driveway which had a skip full of rubbish.

"Who's that?" Kai asked without looking inside, a rising string of fizzy knots forming in her tummy.

"Well, you know who it is," he mumbled, not looking at her. "Look, you go inside, and I'll sort this out."

"No, I'll wait out here, thanks."

The girl in the car put down her phone, flung open the car door, rushed round the bonnet in denim shorts and confronted them both.

"Is this your girlfriend, Jason?" she asked with a Spanish accent.

Out of the corner of her eye, Kai spotted Jason scuttling to stand behind the skip, using it as a barrier. *Coward!*

"Did you know he was with me Saturday night?" she hissed, hands on hips.

Kai turned to look at the girl with long black hair, green eyes and pink lipstick. She was pretty. Jason groaned in the background from somewhere in his safe zone. Kai felt a ping in her chest. A little bit like an elastic band snapping from sharp pointed glass. Her breastbone caved in slightly, and she had no doubt that her heart had broken. *Oh no! Not you, Jason. Not you as well.*

"Did you have sex with him?" Kai asked coolly. Spanish-Girl nodded, averting her eyes down to the floor. Calmly, Kai straightened her shoulders, blinked three ritual taps on the leaves of a nearby tree, walked between the girl and the skip, up the doorstep and through the front door.

"You'll go to hell for that!" Jason shot at Spanish-Girl, as he followed Kai into his house. He stood at the bottom of the stairs while Kai scrabbled around in the bathroom for her toothbrush, and the bedroom for her clothes, cramming them all into her sports bag. Unsure whether she should be crying at this point or not, her feet wavered down the stairs to where he blocked her from going any further.

Spanish-Girl was banging on the front door with relentless Mediterranean insanity.

"Oh, why can't she just go away?" he asked the ceiling, anchoring his hands on Kai's shoulders. She stepped away from his grip, her back eager to find the support of the wall. Her legs buckled as she sat on the floor in a crumpled heap, covering her face as a few tears tipped over her bottom eyelashes and meandered down her cheeks.

"Did you kiss her?" It was a silly question, but she wanted him to say no.

"It wasn't like that."

"You said it was just the lads. And you phoned me on the way back – was that before or after you shagged her?"

"I didn't have sex with her, she's lying!"

"You don't have to have sex to cheat on someone, you know?"

"So you believe me?"

"No, I don't believe you! I think it's been going on since Christmas when she left the present on your doorstep. Then when we saw her at the cinema in February and you didn't want to hold my hand in case you hurt her feelings. And I pretended we were just friends to save your back!"

"That's how stupid she is, she didn't even recognise you."

"What's *that* got to do with it?" Kai's legs gained strength and stood her up. She made it to the front door. Spanish-Girl had left. Jason wrapped his arms around her in a final plea to stay.

She would miss his strong arms and allowed the hug for a couple of seconds before peeling away.

"You shouldn't drive like this."

Like what? I feel fine.

"Goodbye, Jason." She opened the front door, climbed into her Astra and started the engine. His bulk strode towards the car with a piece of paper which he stuck to the window, flattening it with his hand. Spanish-Girl had written him a parting love note:

YOU OWE ME £5000, GIVE ME MY MONEY.

Kai looked over the top of the scribble and into his eyes. She shrugged, dissolving all hope he'd had that those words would redeem him. *Typical Jason, borrowing money from a woman.*

She turned the car around at the end of the cul-de-sac, irritated that she had to pass him again to get out of the close, and sped away. Her tummy clenched inwards; she felt sick or needed to empty her bowels – it wasn't clear. Tears flooded her face as adrenalin gave way to reality. She wasn't certain where to drive and grabbed her phone to call her good friend Molly.

"Hello, darling."

"Hey," she sobbed. "Where are you?"

"Kai? I'm at home. What's the matter?"

"Jason's been cheating on me, w-with *that* girl."

"Darling! Come straight over, you can stay with me tonight."

Kai drove through cloudy tear-stained contact lenses to Molly's house.

"Oh, darling." Molly opened the front door and flung her arms around Kai's shoulders, giving her a tight hug for a full two minutes. "That man! Come in, I'll make a green tea." They walked onto the terracotta-tiled floor in the kitchen, and Kai sat at the beech wooden table.

"You're always crying when you're with him. Never happy. What happened, darling?"

Kai relayed the events, while her phone on the table vibrated with missed calls and nonstop texts.

"Is that *him* trying to get hold of you? Turn it off, darling. Just don't answer it."

"But I want him to know why I left."

"You haven't got anything to say to him." Molly placed the mug of green tea on a coaster and gently slid it across the table in front of Kai. "And he'd have to be really thick if he doesn't know why you left! He doesn't need to know where you are, darling, and you certainly don't owe him an explanation. You don't have to make him understand anything. He's a cock."

"He *is* a cock." Kai exhaled and relaxed her shoulders for the first time in two hours. She wrapped her hands around her steaming mug and pulled her knees up to sit cross-legged on the chair. "He'll probably go round to the house."

"Darling, stay here for a couple of nights. Gavin's away until the weekend. Saturday morning he's back, so chill out here for a bit. I have a spare toothbrush, you can borrow some knickers and" – she nodded to Kai's clothes – "we can put a wash on."

"OK, thanks. If you don't mind." Kai looked around the newly tiled kitchen and out of the window to the canal at the bottom of the peaceful garden to where Molly had moored her narrowboat. Molly had lived on a boat for eight years. When she'd got fed up with her long hair and had made the spontaneous decision to chop it all off, she had walked into Gavin's hairdressers, fell in love with his scissor skills and curious curly moustache, and two weeks later had moved in … boat and all.

After a shower and a hot chocolate, they climbed into bed. Drained from the overthinking and replaying of events, they slept the whole night. In the morning, Kai switched her phone on and deleted Jason's texts before she read them.

"You can *do* this, darling." Molly kissed her goodbye and left for work.

Kai drove home, gingerly inspecting the nearby street for Jason's van. The road was clear. Parking the car, she went inside and called in sick for the next two days. They'd have to arrange cover themselves or cancel the lessons – she'd be out of there soon anyway and the monotones of Greyton Pools wasn't her problem anymore.

While the kettle was boiling, she opened the French doors from the living room to the garden. A sudden wave of tears washed her face. She stood for a moment holding the handle for support as that familiar feeling wrenched her gut.

In the garden, she watched the neighbour's silver birches sway to soothe her cramped stomach and slow her mind. She opened the studio doors and windows and changed into her painting clothes, tears dripping onto the newspaper, dispersing blobs absorbed by the print.

She looked down at the canvas and sniffed, wiping her nose on one of the rags. She could finish this painting today, and if it dried for Sunday she'd take it to Bayswater. At least she could get a day's work in before heading back to Molly's tonight.

She didn't have her usual zest for painting today. The passion was dulled by images of Spanish-Girl with hands on hips and Jason's cowering stance behind the skip. *Twit.* She felt sorry for Spanish-Girl. Kai had been in her position so many times, thinking she was special then growing frustrated because he wouldn't answer her calls or texts. He could never finish his idea of a relationship, always leaving his options open, so when he got bored with one, he could flit to another. Girls would never know if they were coming or going, wondering why on earth it felt extremely hard to leave. They were blind to the emotional manipulation, falling in love with a gaslighting narcissist. Guys like that loved causing drama and exerting control, crushing you to a point where you believed it was your fault. They stayed away long enough so just when you thought you were getting back on track, they appeared with charming apologies of poison.

Kai finished blending the reds and yellows and remembered she hadn't had a drink since first thing. She took a break. In the kitchen, clicking the lever to boil the kettle for the second time, screeching tyres drew her attention to the window. Her eyes flashed outside to a speeding silver shark. It swerved two wheels up on the pavement and jolted to a stop. Kai froze. The driver door flung open, and Jason jumped out. She ran to the back garden to lock the gate, but didn't have time to close the studio, *damn!* She quickly pulled the French doors closed, turned the key and drew the vertical blinds so he couldn't see in.

The doorbell rang. Kai listened to impatient footsteps run the length of the house then back again. He pressed the bell, this time in a frenzied overlay of ringtones interrupting each other. He banged on the door with his fist. Kai positioned herself in the living room away from view of the letterbox.

"I know you're in," he roared through the flap. "Your car's here … and your studio is open. Open the door or I'm gonna kick it down."

When the flap closed, Kai tiptoed into the kitchen, grabbed her keys and wondered what to do. There was no doubt he would obliterate the door.

"I just want to talk to you," he said, his tone now more conciliatory.

Kai opened the front door as narrowly as possible and slipped out through the gap as fast as she could, closing it firmly behind her. She turned to face him.

"You know I didn't have sex with her?"

"Oh, that makes it alright then!" She stood with her arms folded tight across herself.

"I had already asked her a while ago to come with me when you and I weren't together, but then—"

"You make up and break up to suit *you*. Then you can see who you want in between and say, 'Oh, we weren't together!' Well, it doesn't fly with me anymore. We're done!" Kai hoped she could make it back into the house as quickly as she had come out. Sliding the key into the lock, she paused and turned to look at him, checking that he wasn't close behind. He stayed rooted on his spot, tight-mouthed, watching. Without taking her eyes from his, she crossed her left arm over her right shoulder, fumbling to find the key behind her. From this awkward position, she gave the key a quarter twist, praying it would open the door. A clicking sound released the lock, and the door eased ajar as she stepped backwards up the step. With her fingers still on the keys and her arm across her neck, her efforts to pull the key from the lock were clumsy. She wasn't at the right angle. She hesitated. In the half second it took for her to turn around and snake the key out of the lock, Jason propelled forwards, bundling Kai into his arms.

He bowled her inwards as he bulldozed into the gap, revolving them both clockwise for one full turn. She flustered, trying to figure out what was happening, her back tucked neatly into his chest. Her feet scrabbled to grip the laminate floor, but it was too slippery. Her hands desperately found the walls either side of the hallway to create some resistance, trying to push him backwards out of the front door, but she could never block this bull of a man. He opened his arms to release her, shoved past and turned to face her square on. The air was thick with danger.

She wondered whether to step outside and lock him in, but didn't want him alone in her house. She stayed where she was and closed the front door behind her.

They glared at each other in the hallway.

"Can't we just talk? I don't want to be with her," he grated the words through gritted teeth.

"So what was the five grand for?"

"I needed it desperately to keep the house. I was gonna lose the house," he said, anger lacing his tone.

"It's not my business anyway." Kai waved dismissively and bravely pushed past him into the living room. "Please go and leave me alone."

"It's alright for you, you don't know how stressful it is nearly losing your house. She helped me out!" he snarled, coming closer.

She looked at him, tormented by his knack of turning every argument around. *How is losing your house* my *fault!*

"But you wouldn't understand that, would you?" he bellowed, stepping even closer. He grabbed the back of her jeans by the belt with one hand, tucking his fingers into the top, and yanked her upwards. Kai's feet left the floor and she folded forwards at the waist, arms dangling so that her fingers brushed her toes. He shook her like a ragdoll before throwing her on to the sofa to land face-down.

Baffled, she wriggled round to lie on her back. His face was level with hers as he bent down, his lips curled around his teeth. She searched his eyes for any clues … they were a hard frosty blue; she couldn't recognise him. For the first time, she felt defenceless.

"I'm fucking warning you," he spat, spinning her round so her legs swung off the sofa, now resting on the ottoman, her back dipping in the gap between. She tried to kick him in the nuts but missed as he backed away.

Hot helpless tears stung her eyes as she sat up, sliding her bottom properly onto the sofa, pulling her knees up to her chest and wrapping her arms tight around her shins.

"Leave me alone," she whispered, afraid to speak any louder as the quiver in her voice would show her weakness … and he thrived on that.

"Oh, I'll leave you alone!" He marched into the kitchen, opened the cutlery drawer, pulled out the forks and spoons, and threw them on the floor. "But you're not having these," he hollered through the clatter, taking a handful of sharp knives.

Kai followed him. "I need those, you can't take my knives! I have lodgers!"

He glared at her for a moment, then strutted to where she stood in the kitchen doorway, positioning himself to her right. His breath was heavy, his shoulders hunched, his face a furious red.

He kicked her right leg forward, dropping her bottom to the floor as her left knee bent. It was quick, but her left hand shot down to break some of the fall. She pressed into the sole of her stable left foot and stood up as quickly as she went down. Jason crashed the knives to the floor, wrapped her arms behind her back so he could hold both her wrists in one hand and grabbed her throat with the other. He held her tight, pressing her against the wall. Kai couldn't move or speak, the upward tilt of her chin aching the back of her neck. He looked as though he might crack her skull with his head, his hot angry breath millimetres away from her mouth. He held her for two minutes, though it felt like twenty – then released his brutal hand from her windpipe. She backed up the stairs and sat on a step, massaging her larynx. His hands flew to his head as he miraculously snapped out of his rage. He looked at her through the white-painted banisters.

"Kai! I'm … I'm so sorry!" He made his way round to the bottom of the kite-shaped staircase.

She stood up, using the advantage of being three steps above him to give her the taller height. "You can leave now." She spoke with a coolness that comes with defeat.

He opened the front door and almost ran out, leaving it wide open. Kai stood very still for a few minutes, staring at the mess on the floor. She looked at the knives; she'd only used a kitchen knife once before to do it but preferred the scalpel she kept upstairs.

She picked herself off the staircase, gently closed the front door and gathered up the contents of the drawer. Previously, she would have run upstairs to do it immediately, but she'd been working on creating space between thought, feeling and reaction. Placing the cutlery back into its correct compartments was buying some time … or delaying the inevitable.

A heaviness gripped her shoulders like cold lead. She was worthless. She was to blame.

Kai hauled her shaky self up the stairs as a gaping feeling ripped at her stomach. She felt sick. Looking out of her bedroom window, there was no sign of his van. He wasn't coming back. Despair arose not at the thought of never seeing him again, but at the forthcoming cycle she couldn't seem to break. Tears flowed to the point where she doubled up over the sink in her en suite, convulsing – but didn't vomit. She closed her eyes to smooth the crinkles of her buckling contact lenses over her sodden eyeballs.

She opened her bedside table drawer, took out the light-blue plastic handle and peeled open the foil covering the end that had been wrapped and unwrapped so many times. She liked to look at it first, the shiny metal blade seducing the addict in euphoric promise, easing her muddled mind to a sharp focus.

Her body was numb. She lay the blade flat in between her old scars, choosing an unmarked piece of flesh.

Tipping the sharp edge of the blade onto the skin and applying pressure, she dragged it slowly on the inside of her forearm towards the elbow. The skin sliced open; tiny red blobs started to appear on the dermis and gather in the middle of the slit … *There I am!* She sliced again on a new part. As the blood pooled into the gash, a rush of endorphins whizzed around her body and into her head.

Lifting her arm and closing her eyes, she placed her mouth over the wound to gently suck. It tasted like she'd just saved her life.

She inhaled – an ascending breath to dissolve the boundaries of physical form – and seemed to float to another dimension. On the outbreath, she sailed to a timeless space of pure energy.

She stayed like this for a few moments with her eyes closed, shoulders loose, and felt a deep connection to peace.

With new strength and a clear head, she tiptoed into the en suite and placed the cuts under cold running water. Kai watched diluted blood swirl against the white ceramic, flushed away like a bright cadmium-red watercolour. It was still bleeding. Toilet roll would stick to the open wound – she needed a gauze to place under a bandage or Steri-Strips. She gently pushed the skin back together and held it for a while. Globs of blood oozed out. No doubt this would form a keloid scar to match the others.

Opening the cupboard under the sink, she took out a bottle of TCP, dabbed it on a cotton pad and wiped around the wounds. Keeping the skin together while trying to cleanse as much as she could with one hand, she pressed down firmly and suffered the sting.

Feeling grounded, she went downstairs, folded a piece of kitchen towel in half, dampened it under cold water and wrapped it around the cotton pad. She opened a drawer, took out the Sellotape and picked at the end, sticking it to the edge of the worktop and cutting a few strips with the scissors. She taped over the kitchen towel tight enough for it not to come loose, and not too tight so that her fingers turned blue ... *done* that *before!*

Exhausted, she went to the living room, curled up on the end of the sofa and fell asleep.

Chapter Ten

It was half-seven in the morning. Kai woke from her sleepy ball to seven missed calls and twelve text messages from Molly.

KAI DARLING, WHERE ARE YOU? ARE YOU COMING TONIGHT? OK, IF I HAVEN'T HEARD FROM YOU BY 9AM, I'M COMING ROUND TO SEE IF YOU'RE OK. XXXX

She quickly replied to the last text.

HEY. SO SORRY, I FELL ASLEEP.

Kai looked down at her jeans. There was a red patch on her outer thigh. She sat up to a slight soreness on her left forearm blobbed with dried tissue.

I'M OK. THANKS SOO MUCH FOR THE OTHER NIGHT AND LOOKING AFTER ME. I'LL TEXT YOU LATER. LOVE YOU. XXXX

She picked up the rest of the kitchen towel, put it in the bin and made her way into the kitchen. It had bled more than she'd thought this time, and the Sellotaped tissue hadn't held together.

Turning on the tap and holding her arm through lukewarm tumbling water, she eased off the dried tissue and fluff from the cotton pad. *What day is it? Friday – oh no!* She was supposed to be working at the club tonight. How could she hide her sliced arm? She wouldn't look very sexy with a bandage over it … perhaps it would be dark enough and no one would notice. *Oh, and teaching swimming too! Arrrrrhhh!* Though it wouldn't have made any difference if she'd thought of that at the time; the rapture of the blade would always crush any rationale.

She made herself a hot chocolate, sat on the sofa and looked out to the serene sway of the silver birch trees in the neighbour's garden. The slow, gentle sweep hushed any ruminations of yesterday. Wrapping her hands around the mug, she looked down at her arm. The fresh cuts, red and soft before the scab, soothed her bruised emotions.

Taking her drink into the garden, Kai unlocked the studio door, changed into her painting jeans and chose a short-sleeved T-shirt to keep her wounds from rubbing on any material. The surface of the canvas she'd been working on was touch dry … good, a new addition for Bayswater.

There were a few blank canvases declaring their empty depths, pleading for her attention. Pulling on a new pair of surgical gloves, she set to work, moulding meringue-shaped mounds of modelling paste sculpted by the palette knife. Covering three canvases and setting them aside, she dived into her box to choose today's colours. She'd mix a turquoise using Pthalo and Cerulean Blue, Lemon Yellow, Titanium White, and perhaps a touch of Viridian Green. Emerald Green would provide the iridescence, while Prussian Blue would quietly thunder his dark depths of contrast in silent sovereignty. The enigmatic leveller.

With all glass beads mixtures complete in their tubs and covered with cling film to save drying out, she took a break while the modelling paste hardened on the canvases. In the kitchen, she tipped her now "cold" chocolate down the sink and poured a glass of water.

She checked her phone for any messages from Molly and found an email from Jason instead.

KAI,

I AM SO SORRY FOR WHAT HAPPENED YESTERDAY. I HAVE NEVER DONE THAT BEFORE, AND I DON'T EXPECT YOU TO FORGIVE ME. I'M SORRY I LOST MY TEMPER. I WILL NEVER DO THAT TO YOU AGAIN. PLEASE GIVE ME ANOTHER CHANCE TO MAKE IT UP TO YOU.

JASON.

She ignored it. Then deleted it and walked back to the studio. *Twit!* Her phone silently vibrated, ringing in her hand. It was Molly.

"Kai, darling! Where are you? And what are you doing? Am worried about you!"

"Hey. No need to worry. I'm at home, just about to start painting in the studio. How are you, what you up to?"

"I'm at work, darling, sooo boring! Have you heard from him? I haven't seen you since Thursday morning, what's been happening?"

Kai sat on the newspapers and leant her back on the wooden box of goodies. She disclosed yesterday's episode, neutralising the destruction with numerous rounds of three blinks on the blank white walls of the studio – accompanying them every now and then with three taps, jerky backward shoulder movements and thigh parting. She didn't mention the cutting.

"You should report him to the police, darling! He's a bully and that's abuse."

"I can't be bothered with the hassle – plus that might make him worse."

"Well, you can stay here for a few nights, Gavin won't mind. Are you working tonight at the club?"

"Yes, I am – am hoping it will take my mind off things."

"Well, take it easy, darling, and I'll catch up with you soon."

Wiggling her fingers back into the gloves and peeling back the cling film from the pots, Kai scooped out the best turquoise she had ever created. A luscious land of eternal aquamarine to dissolve all dilemmas.

She turquoised her way around the canvases and painted into the late afternoon. Today, blues splashed around the surface and found their way like jubilant water. Prussian deepened the composition with inward expanse to captivate viewers as they peered into his profundity.

It was five o'clock. Time to down tools, de-glove and shower. After her ablutions, Kai moisturised all over, taking care around her lacerations. She grudgingly brushed eyeshadow on her eyelids, clogged her eyelashes, botched her cheeks and messed her lips. Throwing a short dress, hot pants, a couple of sexy tops and underwear into her rucksack, she headed for the club.

It was the usual scene. Loud music. Barmaids toying with doormen. Girls waiting. Guys arriving. Sexy dances. The night was full of fun and hard work.

"You know what, Kai? I'm a bum man," stated Kai's current catch with a subtle lisp as he sat down on the red leather chair, opening his legs. "Can you turn around so I can watch your ass?"

"Of course." Kai was delighted she didn't have to give him sexy looks throughout the dance, dangling her nipples a millimetre from his watering mouth. She turned away from him and peeled the straps of her black dress over each shoulder and rolled the top half of her dress to her waist. She frittered around like this for a while, pulling the dress up from the bottom to tease him with her bare cheeks. Bending down, she gathered the material in her hands at her hips together with her G-string, rolled them off her buttocks and dropped them to her ankles. Stepping over the tiny bundle and sliding it to one side with her black heeled shoe, she turned back to look at him. His brown eyes sparkled; his top lip tucked into his bottom lip. He shifted position, preparing for something he'd been waiting for all week. She circled her hips in this bent stance and reached her right hand round to stroke her bum, drawing rings with her index finger, moving closer to the centre of her butt cheeks. Without looking at her, he brought his thumbs together side by side and moved his hands away from one another a few times as though parting a crowd, motioning her to open her cheeks. She placed her middle finger at the tailbone and slid it down between two peach halves until it disappeared, then slowly traced it back up to the top. Widening her stance, she began to part her cheeks, rolling them around in each hand. He appeared to be in his heaven, eyes glinting, obsessed with the flash of her arsehole.

She stood up for a few moments to ease her back. The song had come to an end and Bum-Man was rolling his hand forward to indicate another dance. Kai lowered her chest again to resume the posture. Her eyes met DJ Smooth's across the club, who put his thumbs up and laughed as she playfully rolled her eyes to say *this is an easy one.*

Kai looked back at Bum-Man and noted his excitement. She licked her middle finger and rubbed it over the bumpy mound.

"Rrrmmff," he rumbled, changing position in his chair and looking a little closer. *Guys are hilarious!* His smile was coy.

Standing up every so often to soothe the ache in her lower back, Kai danced for another three tracks. On the third – slightly bored – she peered into the adjacent netted cubicle and recognised a big pair of jiggling boobs. She couldn't quite work out where she'd seen them before and looked down the body past the hairless triangle between the thighs. She felt familiar with that, too, though still couldn't place it in this context. When Kai's eyes trailed down the slim legs and skinny anklebones, there was no mistaking the girl. Kai looked up to see Caren grinning and waving. Kai mouthed a long, dawning O, threw her head back and laughed.

When the song finished, Kai turned to Bum-Man who smiled as he took his wallet out of his shirt pocket. He watched her get dressed and handed her fifty quid.

"Thanks. I really enjoyed that," he said without making eye contact.

"It was a pleasure dancing for you." She meant it. There was something innocent about him. He was calm, balanced and quietly confident, not cocky and drunk like half the men.

She led the way out of the curtain, said bye to Bum-Man and walked to the bar. An arm snaked around her shoulder and she turned into Caren's embrace. They swayed in each other's clasp for a while, giggling.

"Sooo *this* is Friday 'me time'!"

"Yep!" Caren replied with a grin. "I was brought up in Ealing, love this place. Matt and I used to come here when it was just a normal nightclub, years ago."

"Oh, cool. How long have you been working here?"

"Started a couple of years ago. Matt will be along later – he comes occasionally for a free dance or two."

"Oh, he knows about you doing this? He doesn't mind?"

"Yep, he knows and doesn't mind at all – you could dance for him if you like. Or we could do one together – he'd love that!"

"Sure, that'd be great." Kai admired Caren's nonchalance at her husband watching naked women. "Why didn't you say anything when I told you about the audition?" She would have a different slant each time she looked at those boobs in the swim changing rooms from this point on.

"I wanted to surprise you. It's a different life here, away from the mundane chores, kids, dogs, teaching. You can be who you want. I'm not a mum, or a wife or a swimming teacher. On Friday nights, I'm Billie-Jay … I'm freeee!" She lifted her chin towards the sky, briefly closing her eyes, then turned to the barmaid and asked for two bottles of water. "There's usually a guy who spends a bit of cash with me on a Friday." She scanned the club. "But doesn't look as if he's here tonight."

Kai looked at Caren's plastic high heels and was just about to ask what the deal was, when DJ Smooth announced, "Welcome … Billie-Jaaaaay!"

"Oooh, that's me, gotta go. See you later." She handed Kai a bottle of water.

"Thanks – have fun!"

Billie-Jay slunk off to the stage where she twirled, climbed, stripped and wriggled around on the floor. Kai smiled. Parents at the pool had no idea. Hardly anyone who knew them had any idea.

Kai looked around for her next dance. Bum-Man was indulging in another bottom; Billie-Jay was seducing two men from the stage ready to procure when she had finished her routine; and the African girl had taken off her shoes as it was more comfortable to manoeuvre around men's legs when she was barefoot.

Kai stayed at the bar, sipping water, and observed the scene.

There weren't many men in the club. In fact, the dancers outnumbered the clients this evening, which meant a lot of tension as girls raced to the next available man. Lots of dirty looks were exchanged, and men didn't care who got to them first. They reached into their pockets and bought the girls drinks. They had conversations with their boobs and downed their beers. Girls would stand up and lead the way, and guys followed like lap dogs.

Kai spotted a man sat on his own, after his pal had been led off by Lola.

"Hi," she greeted him as she sat down.

"Hi," he responded. "I'd love a chat. I'll pay you to chat. I don't want a dance."

Oh, it gets better! She liked the sound of that – getting paid to *chat.* Did that mean the chat lasted three minutes? Would she stop halfway through the conversation and ask for payment?

"Is Stephanie working tonight?" he asked. Kai had met Stephanie, aka *Isabella* from Venezuela. Fair skin, black hair, green eyes, slim build, married with two kids. Her husband also came to watch her dance now and then.

"No, I don't think she's in tonight. Probably with her family."

"What family?" He pricked up, looking as though his whole life had just shattered. "She told me she was single." He looked deeply hurt. Kai stopped herself from laughing at his gullibility.

"Oh, perhaps there are two Stephanies," she said, trying to save his embarrassment.

"She lied to me! We got on really well. Why would she do that?"

Surely guys aren't this callow? The song came to an end, and he took a ten-pound note and handed it to her, thanking her for her honesty. She felt sorry for him.

"Thanks." She folded it away into her purse, making a sharp getaway with a departing squeeze of her hand on his shoulder.

More guys were arriving, evening out the numbers. Kai was called to the stage, where she danced to her tunes. She braved a few more moves on the pole and turned herself upside down, making it up as she went. On her second track she tried to climb the pole a little higher, though the grip on her black suede shoes did not keep traction with the shiny metal. *Ahhhh – the plastic shoes!* She styled out the slide – men were either too drunk to notice or too engrossed in boobs and pussy.

When Kai finished on the stage and was climbing back into her blue minidress, Billie-Jay came and stood beside her.

"Come on, Matt's here – and he's brought a crowd!" She linked Kai's arm and guided her towards the group of fifteen guys who sat with her husband.

"Alright, how's it going?" they cheered.

"All good, bit slow tonight," Kai said, slinking into a red tub chair.

"Well, let's speed it up a bit then." One of the guys lit up. "Come and give me a dance. I'll buy you a drink after and we can have a chat. Love your dress. I'm Reuven by the way."

"Thanks!" Kai perked up.

Reuven took her hand and led the way, as though he'd done this a thousand times. She followed his V-shaped back and short dark hair, cut very close to his head. All the usual chairs were taken, and he towed her up the step that led to the overflow section. Before he sat down, he whispered in her ear, "I know we're not allowed to touch the girls, but I used to work here as a doorman, so they know me. I don't think anyone saw us anyway." Kai relaxed. He seemed pleasant and friendly, probably charming all the girls with that line.

"There's not enough doormen to watch this part of the club; they stay in the main bit." His eyes twinkled with a knowing that she did not seem to know about.

Diamond's wriggly hips were leading one of the guys from Matt's crew up the lighted step and straight into a cubicle, while Lola had secured another. Billie-Jay preceded her beloved who followed behind singing the words "what a wicked thing to do" along with Chris Isaak. Reuven sat on a red leather armchair, veiled by the gold nets.

It seemed darker on this side of the club. No doormen. No bar. No barmaids. A shady laid-back vibe.

Reuven parted his legs and motioned Kai to step in between. She mouthed the second line of the chorus with a silly pout. Reuven was horny – she could see that through his trousers. Kai twirled to face away from him and eased her dress over her buttocks, dropping it to the floor. She looked across to see Billie-Jay sitting in her husband's lap, her back to his chest, riding his jeans. He was kissing her neck as she snuggled her shoulder under his chin.

Kai looked over into Lola's cubicle where she sat facing her guy, astride his groin, knees bent on the leather chair either side of his thighs, brushing her smooth pale skin over his T-shirt. Every now and then, shifting her weight into her knees and raising her buttocks off his lap, she teased his face with her hard nipples until he gave in, nibbling and sucking like a hungry baby, his hands firmly wedged underneath his bottom. *Hmmm ... a little more flexible on the regulations this side of the club.*

Kai slid her thumbs into the tops of her knickers and wound each side round and round, flashing the top of her bum before pulling the sides down so they rested at the top of her thighs, low enough so when she turned back to face Reuven, he could see her shaved lips. She gestured for him to pull down her knickers. He sat up closer, placed one hand on the middle of her thong at her inner thighs, and pushed it down to the floor, his head close to her mound. She stepped out of her knickers, holding on to his shoulders. *So much easier when you have something to hold on to!*

Reuven sat up slowly, brushing the backs of her legs with his hands, and planted a kiss on both thighs before easing backwards into the red worn leather. He gently pushed his knees in between her legs, widening her stance to straddle his thighs.

She stepped her feet on the floor either side of his ankles and began to dance, allowing parts of her body to touch his. It was very liberating, snapping the rules. She wriggled up and down, drawing circles with her hips where she sat on his jeans and put her mouth so close to his, he stole a kiss. She didn't pull away. It was a proper kiss. As Chris Isaak faded to the end, their kiss deliquesced.

"Hmmmm … that was lovely," he said with his eyes closed, leaving his head in the same position for a few more seconds. "I'd love another dance."

Kai danced another four songs before leading him back to the main area, where the club was now full. Reuven ordered them both a drink and sat close, engaging her fully with his conversation as it flowed into the art world, hitting upon her favourite artist, Rothko.

"When you sit in his room at the Tate, you want everyone to be quiet and leave. But then you enter a space where the vibration of the paint blurs the boundaries and invites you to float within its depths," he said, taking the words out of her mouth. She had sat in that room many times – her spirit crossing the black mauves of Rothko's paintings; but there were always so many people making too much noise for it to go deeper. She'd wished she'd been the only one in that room so she could lie spread out on the floor and dissolve.

"Oh, I love that room! I could sit there for hours absorbing their magic. They have an energy that transcends this dimension." It was wonderful to talk to someone who could align with Rothko, understanding his depth.

"The Seagram Murals. Did you know he originally painted those for a restaurant in New York?"

"Oooo, yes, I *did* know that." Kai was intrigued and found talking to this guy far more compelling than wriggling around naked. She watched his lips as he spoke of "how the haze of the inner rectangles seemed to oscillate" – and thought she might kiss his words.

"Yeh." He leant forward to take a sip of his beer then placed it back on the small round table. "The Four Seasons Restaurant in the Seagram building. He decided afterwards that the rich wouldn't appreciate or understand their intensity, so gave them to the Tate instead."

She nodded. "He took his life the same day those paintings arrived at the Tate." Kai guessed Reuven would have known about the overdose but didn't draw attention to Rothko cutting an artery in his arm. She gasped. She'd forgotten about her arm until now and tucked it into her side.

"That's right." He nodded.

"So you know a bit about art?"

"I do." He grinned. "Did a bit of door work on the side with my brother here and there, but to be honest, I've done that for so long I'm bored of it. And you move on and evolve in life. Tastes change and you learn to let go of rigid opinions."

Kai nodded and wondered what on earth he thought of her taking her clothes off for a living! Well, it wasn't exactly a *living*, and she *had* made it clear that she was an artist for all intents … even though she taught swimming, was a life model and a sales assistant. Her heart sank whenever she thought about it.

"You have to *believe* that you can be an artist." He linked in to her thoughts. "And fuck anyone who tells you otherwise!" He picked up his beer and tilted it towards her glass of water. She took her glass and clinked his pint. "People will try and tell you how you *should* be living your life." He took a gulp. "But that's usually because they're jealous and unhappy, blaming *you* for their life choices." He emphasised the end of his sentence, clonking the bottom of his glass on the table, and looked straight into her eyes. "And they're really good at spinning a story that everyone forgets there's another side to."

Kai tipped her face upwards and puffed air down her nostrils, nodding. *Been there!* When she looked at him again, his slightly glazed stare declared a wound that she hoped he would share with her one day.

"We don't have to prove ourselves to anyone." She took his face in her hands, diffusing his tension. "Do you kiss *every* girl who dances for you?" She led him out of his introspection.

“You’re the only one.” She didn’t believe him, but it didn’t matter – this was the land of lies.

“Come on, Reuve!” His mates interrupted their connection. “It’s time to go.”

They both stood up and looked around. The club was emptying.

“I really enjoyed our chat tonight.” Kai looked at him.

“Me too. Will probably see you again.” He bent down to kiss her lips, before following his friends out of the club.

Chapter Eleven

Baker School is running better than she'd thought. Delightful parents to only come on poolside on the last day of term to see how their kids are progressing, and no scowling mothers who hate the sight of you. Only five in a class and no one to tell you how to do the job you've been doing for the last sixteen years. Sometimes, it's not *what* you do – but *how* you do it.

"Great start, you guys," Kai encourages Ben and Grace who have switched from Sea Turtles. Their floats ping out from under their arms as they struggle to keep hold. "Let's take control of these naughty pieces of toast and pop them back under the toaster." Kai tucks the floats under each of their arms. "There you go, one under *that* toaster, and one under *that* one – press down with your levers." She secures their forearms and elbows onto the floats. "And take them all the way across to the other side to spread jam, honey or Nutella!"

The twins, Emma and Jack, have come over from Greyton Pools and are familiar with the pieces of toast. They also have a long bendy sausage under their arms.

Leo is completely new and finds the toast and sausage hilarious.

The Hoop of Magic finishes the lesson, and the kids climb out to meet their mums, dads or nannies, who have returned from wiling away half an hour, and take them off to get changed.

Kai greets the parents and children of the next group, including Laura and her dad, who gives her a huge smile.

"I'll be back in half an hour," he announces to Kai, shaking his hand free from his daughter's tight grip, with the hope of making his five-year-old more independent.

This beginners' group is more confident. They swim without aids, put their faces in the water and don't mind bubbling under every now and then. Freddie (who refuses to wear his hat) and Millie, are the tallest, both standing with feet flat on the floor. Freddie's hair is waist-length like Millie's – who neatly packs hers away under a swimming cap – but Freddie insists on wearing his in a plait, Viking style. Paige, Tommy and Laura happily bounce off the balls of their feet whenever they need to take a break.

By the end of the lesson, bustling bodies arrive to pick up kids, while others descend to drop them off. Kai barely sees Laura's dad as he waves goodbye through the commotion.

The third and fourth groups are competent to swim lengths, working on stroke improvement and stamina. Two lengths front crawl and two back crawl for the warmup, they can't wait to slip their feet into the fins for the first half of the lesson.

Xander and Oscar race each other round to the edge of the pool. As Oscar usually wins each week, Xander has added a decider … the first one to sit on the edge *and* put his fins on is the champion. Xander hasn't lost for three weeks running.

The rest of the group come to join them and follow the new drill of putting their fins on for the warmup, to save time. They all set off at once, fin-speedy. After they complete four lengths, Kai instructs side leg kick, one arm extended under the head, other arm on the side of the body.

"Tummy faces the side; long straight arm under the head, palm faces the floor. Rogan, Xander and Katie, off you go. Shoulder out of the water." She walks along the side, demonstrating as they swim. "Ear on your arm." She puts her ear on her extended arm. "Kick sideways." She scissors her arms. "Oscar and Jess, off you go." They progress through the drills, swapping arms at either end of the pool and finish with full stroke, no fins. Although Jess is the quietest of the group, she is the strongest.

"Can we do diving?"

"For the rings!"

"Handstands!" the girls counter-suggest.

"We can do both," Kai soothes, throwing in the sinkers.

At this deeper end of the pool, the group can fully stretch to an upside-down submerged position. They retrieve the sunken objects to the side, then go back for a handstand.

"I can't touch the floor!" Xander is exasperated as he comes up for air. "I CAN'T DO IT! It's STUPID!" he hollers, as tears threaten his big brown eyes.

"One thing at a time. Let's break it down and do it slowly." Kai calmly guides him through the sequence of a head-first surface dive, with a vertical leg kick at the end and a pull of the arms that lead him down to the bottom. He plants his hands on the tiles and holds the position for over five seconds. He pushes up to the top and shouts, "I did it, I DID IT!"

"I saw you! That's awesome, for six seconds too! Great job!"

The more time Kai spends teaching, the more she notices how children's mental processing, understanding and behaviours are changing over the years. When she first started teaching, hardly anyone had heard of neurodiversity. Now, neurotypical is in the minority.

Xander isn't the only child who throws in an "I hate you" and a "fat pig" every so often. There are at least two children out of every five in her classes who struggle to express what they really want to say. Now and then, "you're not the boss of me" slaps its way across her face, no doubt induced from an overwatched kids' TV programme; and a refusal to do anything at all is not to be taken personally. Kai believes this new medley of personalities was sent to break the archaic schooling system, to inspire and re-educate the educators to bring a contemporary way of teaching.

Consumed by OCD, Kai understands that "fitting in" is never going to be an option. She's intrigued by these fresh minds, similar to hers, that abhor authority and crave freedom. *Some*thing, *some*how, was filtering into their bloodstream.

"Climb out, go and get changed and I'll see you next week." Kai ends the lesson. Xander gives her his weekly cuddle before running to the Spanish nanny, Carmen, who wraps him up in his towel.

The conveyor belt of mums or dads dropping off and picking up kids highlights Kai's childhood with her siblings: drab dance school, strict swim lessons, screechy violin practice, boring

Brownies, jobsworth Guides, frantic football and the serious but very useful St John Ambulance … the cycles of life.

Lessons were over for the day. She would pop to Petal Village once she'd packed up here, to see how the folks were getting on. She hadn't seen them for a while and there was no chance of bumping into her sister anymore, since she had moved away after the falling out.

After saying goodbye to the last of the parents, Kai heaved the handle of the pool cover clockwise. The thick blue vinyl crept across the surface of the water, provoking thoughts that someone might still be in the pool. She checked, tapped, blinked and breathed the pattern of three whilst looking at the wall of the polytunnel, making sure her thighs weren't touching, then sighed at having to do it again. Locking up and handing the keys back to reception, she headed to her mum and dad's.

They were sitting in the garden when Kai arrived at the converted bungalow which had been the family home for many years.

"Ciao, ciao." She greeted them both with a kiss on each cheek.

"Hello, how are you?"

"Good, thanks."

"Ciao. Your hair's wet," her mum said.

"Si, si, been teaching today. How's you guys? What you up to?"

"Oh, just relaxing in the sunshine and some weeding in the flowerbeds." Her dad sat upright, shielding his eyes from the bright sun with his hand.

"I'll put the kettle on. Green tea?"

"Ooo, si, siii, lovely Mummy."

Kai happily sat in one of the garden chairs and tipped her chin up to the sun's rays.

"How's Baker School going?" her dad asked.

"It's OK. Much better than Greyton Pools. Would much rather be painting though."

"Painting doesn't pay the bills."

Kai didn't bite. She took a well-rehearsed strategic ten-second breath which worked miracles, especially when in the company of one's parents. He wasn't being facetious. He seriously meant it. *He's right of course* – painting *paintings doesn't pay the bills ...*

"*Selling* them does," he finished her thoughts out loud.

Well, paintings don't paint themselves! She didn't expect him to understand.

"Heeya we are," her mum timely chirped, with her fabulous Calabrian accent. "There are some cakes too … and biscuits."

"Ahhh, no grazie, Mum – trying not to eat rubbish."

"Ah, c'mon, *one* won't hurt you."

But that was the problem … one *did* hurt when you couldn't stop and ended up eating the whole packet! Kai declined and sat back in the sunshine.

"So what have you guys been doing?"

"We've been working like slaves," was her mum's standard reply. "Weeding there by the summerhouse, and all the borders." She waved generally at the garden. "Dad still pulls out all my flowers because he thinks they're weeds! I don't know *what's* the matter with that man!"

"I do NOT! Those were growing all over the place, then nothing else can grow!"

"Whatchyou talking about? Maria gave us those bulbs a few years ago, and we planted them together."

"Aah!" He tutted. "*You* don't know what *you're* talking about ..."

Kai winced at the name and shivered at the oversized drama that had taken place fifteen years ago. She took her cup of green tea and left her parents bickering easily at nothing.

Strolling barefoot along the garden path paved with Fossil Indian Sandstone, Kai slowed into the warm breeze as it whirled her back to younger days. The huge Swedish-style log cabin that now stood to her left had replaced the old greenhouse where tomato plants grew, tied to canes. Further along would have been the jungle patch of runner beans which Kai and her sister had reluctantly taken turns to water with heavy watering cans.

To the right of the path were a couple of sunken circles about twelve feet apart, where two apple trees once grew, offering a branch to swing from and turn upside down. The trees had once stood like brothers before becoming diseased and chopped down, leaving two dents in the ground that would never heal properly.

Through the conifers and into the neighbour's garden would have been a swimming pool where she had spent countless summers with her brother and sister, splashing around and sunbathing until being called through the hedge to come home for dinner.

She walked a little further to stand underneath the huge oak tree at the bottom of the garden and looked up into his boughs. A resolute feature marking the boundary long before they had moved in. Kai had found comfort in his spreading branches over many years. He rustled his green leaves, enveloping her in his embrace. Above the privet hedge that completed the border of the garden was the best view of all – the field of freedom.

A green escape to a land of wild grass and flowers, where distant conifers, beech, ash and oak trees lined the perimeter, enticing the wanderer to go beyond. The secret passage to the field was through the gap in the hedge where Kai and her brother would have gently brushed past tough twigs during hot summer holidays, to unknowingly connect with nature's energy.

But that gap had overgrown (much to her father's delight) since she'd stopped throwing apples to the grazing horses, so they'd come closer for a stroke … and an unintended nibble on the shrubbery.

Brilliant shades of earthy greens, illuminated yellow from the sunlight, sang the past to her soul.

The circular mound of earth – which had previously contained bonfires – still gathered to one quarter of the field, and was overgrown with weeds. Mum had said that was where homing pigeons were released, and Kai wondered why on earth they flew back to their cages after being set free.

Years ago, when Kai would play in the garden looking for fairies and four-leaf clovers, hot-air balloons would appear through the ether, floating up high in the distance. Occasionally, one would sail close to the rooftops, its colours glowing brighter as its descent delivered a looming shade of mystery and a roar from the dragon's mouth. Kai had prayed for one to land in the garden, but touchdown had always been cleverly deposited in the field, and her heart had deflated with the cascade of the balloon itself.

Pressing her feet into the soft grass cushioning the soles, she felt velvet blades creep into the space between her toes. She turned to look back down the garden to the huge conservatory that spread across the width of the bungalow. A tiny sun lounge with rotting window frames and leaky windows would have taken part of that space. Kai's sister had plausibly told her one evening that it had filled with water all the way to the ceiling, and if she finished her vegetables quick enough, she could go for a swim.

But that wasn't the demise of the sun lounge – it had been resurrected at the end of the garden in true Dad-style. Mouldy wood and flaking paint topped shattered windows; inside stood stacked ladders, planks of splintered timber, broken plant pots, uneven shelves, rusting metal, broken-pronged digging forks … and of course no space in which to get to any of these useless items! *Funny what we hold on to.*

Kai walked to sit with her parents again, who sat in comfortable reticence.

"D'you remember how the garden used to look? With the old shed and greenhouse, and that crumbling wall," she asked, admiring a huge laurel that her mum had planted over twenty years ago. Standing taller than the conifers, it had grown, changed shape, and now stood proud and established.

"Yes, it used to be much nicer before," her mum happily moaned. "It's too much work now, moving all the pots to power-hose the patio. We haven't got the strength anymore – I'd like to get rid of them all." Her mum changed her mind so often, Kai had learnt not to take her seriously … though one day, her mum *had* got fed up with a monumental money plant and murderously chopped it to pieces.

Acers, apple and lemon trees sat comfortably in their heavy terracotta bases, while fuchsia pinks, yellows, violets and off-whites chirped from their pots.

"And the hole in the middle of the garden," her dad added. Oh, she'd forgotten about that. When they had first moved here, the garden had dipped in the centre, where old tyres and rope had been thrown. Her sister used to tease her that they were black snakes.

"Oh my word! That was before Mikey was born! Funny how life moves on."

"And now he's living in America." Her mum still hadn't come to terms with her son's relocation to the States. "And the kids are starting to forget us."

"Ahhh, they won't forget you guys. You speak with them on FaceTime, and perhaps you can visit them soon."

"We'll see. So how's teaching?" her mum asked. "You still teaching part-time?"

Kai shuddered. She didn't class having previously taught for twenty-six hours a week, running alongside painting and producing artwork to subsequently finding and organising exhibitions (many of which charged to hire the space), to then working at the chemist and life-modelling, as "part-time". Those were the words her sister would have spat … which meant she'd been in contact.

"You've spoken to her then?"

Her mum glanced at her dad the way a child does when they can't keep a secret.

"I don't wanna know." Kai rolled her eyeballs up into her eyelids.

"She *is* your sister."

"Anyway, what I was going to say was" – she began neutralising the sudden onslaught of thoughts with her shoulders and thigh spacing – "thanks for everything you've done for us all, putting up with us and working super hard to make this a real family home." She felt her thanks were slightly marred at the mention of her older sibling – her shoulder still wrestling with the intrusion.

"Well, we did what was best for you all," her dad replied, curious as to how his *best* had split two of his offspring.

He had devoted his life to looking after others over many years. Now a retired GP, he kept his marriage of fifty-three years alive by escaping to the allotment and allowing his beloved the freedom to cultivate miles of material into dextrous patchwork. They rubbed along in a way that suited them.

"Well, I'd better be going. Want to get into the studio while it's still light." She hugged them both goodbye with the customary two-cheek kiss and jumped in the car. Before driving away, she checked her phone.

HI KAI, IT'S JAMES, LAURA'S DAD FROM SWIMMING. WOULD YOU LIKE TO GO FOR DINNER ONE NIGHT? XXXX

Chapter Twelve

"It feels different this time," Kai told her therapist. "We've been on and off for over fifteen years, but it's clear our energies just don't mix. They never have, but I guess we both thought it could work one day. We keep trying, but we glide around in circles, repeating the same pattern that neither of us can pop out of. But every time it happens, it's just draining. I'm exhausted all the time … and he is too."

"Yes, extremely tiring."

"And it's driving my OCD mad, can't concentrate on anything, so many thoughts." Kai drew her shoulder blades together and shifted in her seat, making sure there was space between her thighs. By unnecessarily pulling up a sleeve, she disguised the neutralising pattern of three, pointing her right index finger away from her body.

"Tell me about the OCD."

Kai let out a lengthy noise from her throat, sounding somewhere between a groan and a sigh. Anyone who didn't have OCD never really cared to understand the details, and she may as well have been trying to convince them that the Earth was flat.

Whenever she tried to explain it, people lost interest very quickly. It was too banal to comprehend, and their usual response of "Just stop doing it!" would trigger another bundle of neutralisations.

Kai raised an eyebrow, wondering if this was cruising into another clash of opinions.

"Sometimes I think it would be easier if I had the washing hands one, although I'd be needing to find a sink every couple of minutes and my skin would be sore … but at least I wouldn't be doing these silly body movements. If anyone saw me do it, they'd think I was crazy … actually, people who see me *do* think I'm crazy!"

"Do you mind telling me what they are?"

"Well, I have this *shoulder* thing." She demonstrated the shoulder move. "They have to move back at the same time, at the same level … otherwise I may end up lopsided or hunched one day. Or someone close may end up like that. The right one has to move sideways slightly first, not sure why – then they can both go back together."

"Why do you think it moves sideways first?"

"I don't know. It's like it's pushing it away first, so it can move backwards – clean."

"Pushing *what* away?"

"The thing I'm neutralising. And I have to make a space between my thighs when I do it, so they don't end up getting fat and rubbing against each other. I also spread my toes, so they don't end up sticking together one day."

"Why would they stick together one day?"

"I don't know – might get a condition where that could happen."

"And you're stopping that condition happening by carrying out these rituals?"

"Yes. I know it sounds bizarre, and I wish I didn't have to do them – then I could relax – but it's constant. As soon as I hear a horrid word or see something not very nice, I have to neutralise it so it doesn't happen. Same when a grim thought enters my head."

"Like what?"

"Sometimes, when I'm lying in bed at night and I can't sleep, I turn over and place my foot or arms over the edge of the bed. But if a blade came down like a guillotine, it could cut them off. So if later on in life I have to have something amputated, it would be because I hung them off the end of the bed. I've just neutralised both those words by the way; don't like saying them for obvious reasons."

"What, *amputated* and *hung*?"

"Yes, those. Am neutralising them now, too, cos you just said them again." Kai shifted, shouldered and thighed in her seat, at the same time flicking her hand as though brushing away a fly with her knuckles.

"Did you neutralise when *you* said them?"

"Yes. But I knew when the words were coming so it's easier for me to cover up the movements. I've spent many years masking it so I can get through conversations. I think that's why I don't like being in groups of people – as there are too many people saying too many things that I need to neutralise. I end up falling out of the conversation, and it looks like I'm not paying attention ... and I suppose I'm not, because I'm looking for clear surfaces to blink or stare at, silently saying words simultaneously while

I'm doing movements with any part of the body that will get me through it. I'm better in one-on-one situations."

"And you do it while teaching swimming and dancing at the club?"

"Yes, though I seem to disguise it better when other people are around, and when I'm busy, as the mind has to focus more on what I'm doing. I do it all the time. Twenty-four-seven. The only time I don't seem to do it is when I'm asleep … when I finally *get* to sleep!"

"Do you have trouble sleeping?"

"Not actually sleeping, just *getting* to sleep. My eyes have to close on a clean, clear space on the wall. No picture frames, no windows, no wooden furniture – and it depends what's on the other side of the wall too. The duvet cover is safe to close my eyes on – but not the pillow … because I watched a film with a horrible ending – so no pillows. I can blink, neutralising in the pattern of three, for about twenty minutes! It's *so* consuming. There are certain areas on the bedroom walls to override the thoughts, but that means those particular spaces are used for just that. If I turn over and another thought intrudes, I may use another space but if it's not suitable, I have to turn back to look at the original area but on a slightly different line, neutralise again and then turn back in the hopes no more thoughts bombard my brain before I get to close my eyes."

"Sounds very debilitating. Why would a space not be suitable, and why no picture frames, windows or wooden furniture?"

Kai inhaled in anticipation at having to say words she routinely avoided. Conceding on the exhale, she prepared to conceal the flinches and all involuntary actions that crippled her daily.

"I often do the rituals on a picture as it can be contained in the frame. Two blinks close together and the third further away. Sounds easy, doesn't it, but it has to be just right. It can't come too close to the edge of the frame, cos it might leak out into the room. And it can't touch the edge of the frame if it's made of wood. It can't be on a window as people fall out of windows, and it can't be on wooden furniture as wood signifies coffins and I watched a couple of horrid things on TV which were very disturbing and I don't want that to happen." Her right shoulder shot out to the side before both shoulder blades pulled together behind. She made sure her thighs weren't touching and waved the invisible fly away six times or more. "I don't watch TV anymore, but if it's on and I'm round a friend's house or at the folks, I usually do the blinks on the frame of the TV. It's often accompanied with my finger and thumb running along the frame from where I'm sitting, so it's in the air – but TV frames are so thin these days, it's difficult to contain it on the edge without virtually touching the wall behind it or the screen itself."

"So it looks like you're pointing to the TV?"

"Yes, it looks ridiculous!" Kai laughed. "Like I'm measuring something in perspective between my finger and thumb. If I feel someone can see me, I do it with just the stares and blinks instead, though my foot may move slightly in the same way, or I hide my hand so the fingers do it in a limited way; so I stare in three places, two close together and the third further away – I find a way around anything. However, I can't *always* mask it, as the trigger may be too big or alarming. I slide my head backwards so I'm moving away from whatever it is, in time to the three taps or blinks. If my head touches the surface behind, that means I've gone too far back, which means I may get stuck in a room or somewhere where I can't move backwards. Then I'll be trapped. So I have to leave that extra space to escape if I ever need to. It's not just for me, it's for anyone in my family too. I can tame it, but the more you repress it, it seems to come back double later on."

"Ye-ess, what you resist, persists."

"Hmmm … that does seem to be the case."

"And you said you spoke to a psychologist about this before? Did he help you?"

Kai nodded. "We did exposure therapy … but it was too intense. He tried making me watch the beginning of a horror movie because I'd said I didn't like them – so he thought that would be good to use as it would set me off."

"Yes, a trigger. What happened?"

"Well, I looked away and neutralised with my eyes and hand, and he asked me what was going on in my head. I told him I was saying 'not horrible, not horrible'. So he told me to say the opposite – horrible, horrible. Though it was all a little too much. Even now, I'm neutralising it while I tell you. CBT really did work, though it's something that you have to do every day – and, like most things, I lose interest after a while. But I know it helps."

There was a long pause as Kai eased her body back into a natural position, free of joint strain, rigid muscles and bothersome eye movements. Her breath let go of its fatiguing pattern and she sat still.

"I can't blink on large or disabled people because it's like I'm absorbing them into me, and I or anyone in my family may end up like that one day. Same for anyone who's nasty or stands for things against others. I don't like any violence or hearing about it – yes, I just neutralised that."

"What would happen if you didn't nullify it?"

"Then it could happen."

"Ye-ess," said Jane. "I suppose it's like the story of a man who is madly waving his arms around his head looking peculiar. When someone asks him what he's doing, he replies, 'I'm keeping the elephants away.' The other man says, 'But there *are* no elephants!' To which the first man says, 'I know, I know – see? It's working!'"

Kai giggled and threw her head back. "Hah, yes! It's *exactly* like that!"

"Your day sounds quite tough to get through, doing this all the time."

"Yes, that's why I think I was meant to be an artist. I love the solitary life because I can stay in control. Perhaps that's why I find relationships complex, because we make ourselves vulnerable and enter a world of uncertainty."

"Yee-ess, the only thing you can be sure of in life is death."

"And taxes … unless you live in Dubai, of course."

"Where did the pattern of three come from?"

"I have no idea. I think because *two* taps could cancel each other out. One of my friends, Hannah, is the other way around – everything has to be in twos. Last year, her boyfriend was decorating the spare room, and he put three strips of wallpaper up. She was so distressed that in the middle of the night she got up and ripped the third strip down." She took a deep breath. "It works the other way too," she continued. "So if something good happens or I see something really wonderful, I want to make it last forever. I'm not as demonstrative with this one anymore, as

I can manage it better. So neutralising something bad with three taps, blinks or stares is usually in descending height, and on the outbreath, so I'm not breathing it in, and I have to be careful not to get to the bottom of the breath – as I may be in a situation one day where I can't breathe properly – so I leave some extra space to carry on breathing after the ritual is complete." She paused.

"Go on," Jane said.

"When I hear or see something wonderful, the three taps or eye patterns go upwards on an inhale; again, making sure I don't get all the way to the top. It's like the descent for the bad things moves it away, and the ascent for the good things will make it last longer or forever; things get smaller into the distance as they move away from you, so it means they're disappearing. They grow bigger as they get closer."

"That must be quite hard to do all in one breath?"

"Yes, that's why it takes four or five goes. Sometimes, I neutralise the bad going down, then think of something good going up so it makes it all OK again. Other times, I have to move forwards where I sit, not all the way, in case of … you know …"

"One day you might get stuck?"

"That's right. Then I move backwards, neutralising as I go, but can't get all the way to the back of the seat, as this means I've reached a limit. So in the time it takes for me to move from extending my head and torso forward to backwards, I need to have done the pattern of three; in fact, let's call it the 'ritual three'. If I haven't done it in time, or I'm not happy with the way it was done, or someone speaks and says something that disturbs it, I have to do it again until it feels right. This now makes me look like I'm rocking back and forth, and people think I am mad.

People think OCD is just a matter of lining things up in a neat line, but a lot more goes on mentally than that. There's a whole inner dialogue that hijacks our heads and possesses our bodies. Sometimes I think I'd be better off not being here, as I could float with the universe free of the turmoil at having to keep myself and everyone safe and well."

"Do you mean taking your life?"

"Yes."

"Have you thought of how you would do that?"

"Yes. The next cut I do will probably be the last. I can picture it too." She rolled up her left sleeve, revealing the most recent healing scars. She had forgotten those and paused for a moment. "It will be here." She drew a line with her right index fingernail from the wrist to her elbow. "I can see it now – and taste it; the skin will part sooo deep and wide – a Crimson River to freedom." She closed her eyes, imagining lying in a pool of her own blood. When she opened them again, Jane wasn't quite sharing the same sense of ecstasy.

"Are you having these thoughts now?"

"No. Need to get the right size blade first. I want to do it in one cut."

Jane acknowledged the latest scars on Kai's arm with her eyes and pointed to them with her head. "Are those new?"

"About a week or so … and no, I don't feel like I want to do it now."

"That's good, because if I thought you were in danger of harming yourself, I would have to …"

"… report it," Kai answered at the same time. "Yes, I know. Anyway, moving on to something more disturbing – I am picking up vibes of my sister being around."

"Ye-esss. You mentioned something about her as you were leaving last time."

"Well, her name appeared on Jason's phone when he stayed round that night – I didn't think too much of it at the time. Then Mum mentioned her the other day when I went to visit them – and you *know* there are no coincidences in life."

"How can you be sure it's your sister?"

"I can't. And there are hundreds of Marias."

"There are. And you have no proof it is her."

"I hope it isn't – don't think I could cope with that right now. Anyway, the father of one of the girls I teach has asked me out to dinner. Think I might go. Need to take my mind off the twit."

"Sounds like it could be what you need."

"Hmmm … I don't know, he seems a bit leery – probably like the rest of them, but let's see how it unfolds."

Chapter Thirteen

James wore blue jeans and a grey polo shirt. His blue eyes seemed to glitter across the chicken niçoise salad on the table.

"So how long have you been teaching swimming?"

"I started fifteen years ago as an assistant at Marlborough School in Saint Albans. A lady ran an afterschool swim club with her husband, and I learnt a lot there. She was great – a little old-fashioned … but super knowledgeable. Greyton Pools, on the other hand – like most council-run centres – have absolutely no idea how to run their sessions. It's all about cramming as many paying customers as possible into a class. It's soo silly."

"And I suppose the kids take longer to move up cos there's too many of them. Some parents are so pushy – you should hear them on the balcony moaning that their child should be moving up to the next stage, and how they want them to be a club swimmer. It's not fair on the kids. I just want Laura to be able to swim."

"For sure. Oh, I can imagine the hostility up there, that whole area needs sageing … while they're all sitting there too!"

James's blue eyes widened. "Oh! You're into cleansing and sageing?"

"Yes, I am. Have crystals too."

"Me too!" He sat up and leant forward. "Couldn't tell the guys at work though, they'd all make fun and think I'm mad – a rufty tufty spiritual *builder?"* He laughed, expertly pricking lettuce, tomato and a piece of chicken onto his fork and securing them with the knife. He paused before taking the mouthful. "I did the first level of pranic healing … have you heard of it?"

"Oooh no, I haven't." She lengthened her spine and angled forwards, impressed with his eating etiquette. "It sounds as though it's a type of energy healing?"

He nodded, finishing the food in his mouth before speaking. "Yeah, it's an ancient art of healing using prana – you know prana? Breath of life? Some people call it chi energy. There's a lot more to it, but I like it because you're not actually touching the person."

"Sounds interesting." Kai relaxed as she watched James chew food with his mouth closed, pleased at not having to feel her skin crawl to the sound of smacking lips. Eating with your mouth open was a non-debatable deal breaker. It sent shivers through her veins, her whole body tingling as her ears fought to block out the noise, only to be set on fire instead. Her goose-pimpled scalp would crackle like the splitting shell of a boiled egg, cracking open the skull, oozing her brain inside out like sticky yolk.

"You could do healing in the evenings," she said. "But I know how hard it is to change from one thing to the other. I used to paint in the day, then cut the creative flow short to teach swimming. Then I'd try and pick up where I left off the next day, but it doesn't really work like that."

"I know! It takes a couple of days to step out of building mode and move into healing. I haven't got time to do that, we're so busy at work. Plus, I have Laura to look after as she's with me full-time."

"Oh, you're a single parent with a full-time job. Sounds tough."

"My mum helps me out and I've a friend who steps in, but yeah, I have complete empathy with single parents who have to work as well."

"Laura doesn't see her mum at all?"

"No. Her mum's had a few problems, and we split up a couple of years ago now." He dismissed his words with a shake of his head. "We don't have anything to do with each other."

"Oh, OK." Kai didn't pry any further.

"So you're a painter?" he asked. "What do you paint?"

"I paint abstract oils on canvas, mixed with different mediums to give texture. Been doing it for years, though tricky to make a living … so I teach swimming to balance it all. Seems to work at the moment."

"Do you do anything else?"

Should she tell him she took her clothes off to add to the living? Why on earth not?

"I've just got some work at a table-dancing club in Ealing, and I do a bit of life-modelling for the art classes at Wattles Abbey College."

"Oh, I live near Wattles, in Emerald Village." If he was disappointed in her money-spinning choices, he didn't show it.

"Ahhh, I LOVE Emerald Village – it reminds me of *The Wizard of Oz*."

He nodded, laughing. "I converted a barn for Laura and me; it's called Crystal Cove. It certainly does have a magical quality. We're surrounded by Scots pines, conifers, horse chestnuts, all sorts of healing trees. It was an old farmyard with horses and meadows. Apparently, they used to hold seances in one of the fields, and all sorts of witchcraft used to take place. Think there were some trapped spirits when we first arrived. I had a drumming lady come to drum them away. You could come and see it one day."

"Sounds good!"

"So where are you relationship-wise at the moment?"

Oh crumbs!

"Er, I've just come out of an off-and-on … don't know what you'd call it really … drama-filled nonsense!" She took a deep breath in, looking upwards for celestial guidance and saw a big scribbly mess instead. "I don't think I want to get into anything new right now."

She liked the cool, easy vibes of James. He was articulate, had the same humour, displayed impeccable eating etiquette, collected crystals, and was good-looking. But she was about to start healing from years of false interest and continuous rejection from Jason and didn't have a clue who she was anymore. She was having fun at the club, keeping shenanigans light to stay in control. James had a depth that she could fall into and share the spiritual realm, but the timing didn't feel right.

With a businesslike wave of his hand and shake of his head, he looked down at his plate to find solace in his lettuce.

"I feel like I need to spend time with me for a while and be on my own for a bit," she said. "The guy I was with was seeing someone else, and I've only just found out about it."

He looked at her with genuine warmth. “Oh no – that sounds horrible.”

“Hmmm, few weeks ago … a long and boring story.”

“Not surprised you want to be on your own for a while. Takes as long as it takes to recover from all the lies … and the *emotional* pain.” He recoiled. “It knocks you down hard.”

“Yes, it does! People say it makes you stronger, but each time it happens, it makes you weaker; it snaps off a little piece from your heart until it finally breaks you.”

“*Each* time it happens?”

Kai eased into James’s tenderness and found herself relaying the events of sixteen years ago …

*

Kai had frustratingly forgotten her canvas that she’d bought in Camden at the weekend and tried for what seemed like the millionth time to get hold of Luke on his mobile phone. It was half past nine on Tuesday evening. She had time to make the hour and a half’s drive up to Oxton and be back in Southampton just after midnight. On the other hand, if she decided to stay the night, she could put a load of washing on and take her time to head back in the morning. She stuffed her laundry into a couple of carrier bags, grabbed her overnight washbag and a clean pair of knickers, announced to her housemates that she’d see them at some point and closed the front door.

Kai tried Luke’s mobile phone one more time as she walked to the car. It went straight to answerphone. Starting the engine, she dialled his landline, but the continuous ringtone was even more exasperating than the robotic voicemail!

It didn't matter. If Luke was home when she arrived, she could surprise him – and if he was out, she'd either stay or drive back down depending how sleepy she felt.

The motorway was almost empty, making the journey light and pensive. She had been with Luke for one and a half years. Met him in a nightclub and had wondered why on earth he was wearing dark sunglasses; grew besotted by his dance moves (impressed that he could see anything at all through his shades); and amidst the flashing lights and smoky air, she'd noticed he was chewing gum at an abnormally high speed.

A mechanic at six foot three, black-brown hair and translucent light blue-green eyes – she remembered his tight blue trousers. Just before mobile phones had stolen the romance, they had written their numbers on serviettes at the bar and danced a few tracks together. She had kissed his chemical lips goodnight, and the rest was … *crazy!*

For one year they clubbed most weekends in London, filling their bodies with ecstasy and speed. Kai was paid to dance the podiums and took more drugs to reach the highs. Finally, she realised that not hitting the usual amount of lengths in the pool the following week or staring into the depths of her blank canvas at uni for three hours meant she needed to either stop the high life or get used to moody, life-numbing come-downs.

She stopped the high life.

Luke didn't.

Kai grew tired of watching his grimaces, rolling eyes and juddering jawline every time they went out clubbing. Free from amphetamines, it was clear their levels of consciousness would never meet, and she began to see him from a broader angle. She hadn't noticed how he managed to spread tomato sauce around his mouth when he bit into his burger, clucking his mouth like he hadn't eaten for a week, nor had she been aware of his compulsive lies and checking out other women.

But she did love him. She could help with his issues of losing his Sri Lankan father when he was four years old, rendering him mute for a year. His alcoholic Scottish mother had brought him up with his two sisters through a selection of men who abused all three of her children. Luke and his sisters were split between foster homes, and they hadn't seen each other for over fifteen years – until the death of their mum three months after he and Kai had got together. She was found dead and drunk at her home, after falling in the kitchen.

Kai pulled into the services, parked near the entrance, got out and stretched from fingertips to toes. The February evening air freshened any haze from the journey, and she quickly ran into the toilets. Service stations reminded her of going on holiday – a last stop before queuing at the ferry port or shuttle – the bustle of excited families eager to leave the grey skies of England. But tonight was the quiet hush of the night shift. She ordered a hot chocolate and took in the surroundings. A lorry driver sat behind his newspaper, a mug of steaming coffee promising to keep him awake another couple of hours. Four workmen wearing hi-vis dived into their burgers, while a couple slotted their coins into the fruit machines by the toilets. A handful of people coming and going, working their own agenda.

Back in the front seat of her black Peugeot 106, she reached into her bag for her mobile phone and dialled again. No answer.

She sat for a while warming her hands around the hot takeaway cup before starting on the road once more. Another forty minutes and she'd be at Luke's. Feeling a little tired now, staying the night and heading south in the morning seemed like a safer option.

Leaving the lights of the motorway, she travelled through bends and hills, mini roundabouts and traffic lights – the dark emphasising her not-so-sharp vision through her contact lenses. Passing Capes Village on her right, she was on the home-straight to Oxton, glad to be on the last road to her final destination. Spotting the church on the corner, she turned right into Saint Martin's Square and parked in the visitors' parking bay.

Stepping out of the car and opening the boot, she grabbed all her bags, locked the doors and headed across the blocked paved car park to number nine. Luke's van was parked in its allocated space outside. The house lights were off. The small triangular panes of glass arranged in a semi-circle at the top of his wooden front door reflected the dancing television lights, flickering through the darkness. A warm tingly feeling spread through her tummy … *Ah good, he's home.*

Untangling her keys through the muddle of carrier bags, she slid the silver Yale into the lock and gave it an awkward turn as the bags swung left to right. She stepped up onto the threshold. Luke was sitting on his usual side of the sofa. She gave him a big smile, bundling through with her bags. The door opened wider to reveal full view of the settee. At the other end sat a girl with long dark curly hair.

A sensation Kai had never felt before crawled over her skin. Possibly, her blood was on fire, as she watched the scene unfold in slow motion. With disturbing calm, she set her bags on the floor in the hallway, noticing the landline had been pulled out of the socket.

Cautiously, she followed her own footsteps into the living room, her heart hammering in her throat. A magnified pulsing that she had no control over pounded through her ears and chest.

She felt lightheaded, as though her feet had left the ground and her body was floating. She obliterated into a billion pieces, her existence suspended in the treacherous air.

Adrenaline swept in, reassembling the fragments.

"Hello," she breathed. "Who are you?"

"I'm … I'm a friend," the girl stuttered, looking in Luke's direction, then back again. "I'm sorry – I didn't know," she lied, hiding behind her hair. Desperate for Luke's input, the girl glanced at him once more, as though he may be able to offer a more justifiable explanation.

Kai turned to look at Luke, who sat in stunned silence, and noticed his trousers were undone.

She positioned herself to stand so close in front of the girl that her hips squared up to the girl's eyes, trapping her where she sat. Kai wanted to believe her, clinging to anything that could lessen the pain – maybe Luke *had* told her he was single.

It made no difference. Kai stepped backwards, pulled her right arm back, clenched her hand into a fist and delivered a right hook. The punch sent the girl sideways. She scrabbled to her feet, screeching,

"Help me, Luke, help me!"

Kai hadn't noticed until now, but the girl had been sitting with a cushion over her lap. As she scurried off the sofa, the cushion fell away, revealing she wasn't wearing any knickers.

The flash of her bare skin around her pelvis and thighs was highlighted by the light from the television. She scuttled round to the side of the sofa, backing herself into the corner at the bottom of the stairs.

"I've got a kid!" she offered hysterically, hoping to stop the frenzy. "I've got a nine-year-old kid!"

Kai flicked her glance to Luke – *you just try and help her! Go on if you fucking dare to get up and help her!* Her rage was strengthening her muscles … she was ready to take them both. Kai turned back to Half-Naked-Girl at the bottom of the staircase. "You'd better get out then if you've got a kid." Kai's voice deepened with surprising measure. She wondered if the girl would risk passing her.

Half-Naked-Girl froze. Luckily for her, Kai now stood in front of Luke who was speechless on the edge on the sofa. Fury possessed her. She pulled up her fists, reached her right arm back and used her hips to power it forward, punching him square in the face. He rocked back on the sofa and tried to get up. His head was at a good level for her five-foot stance. She watched him intensely as he came forward, his breath spiced with alcohol. Her fist cracked him again, tossing him to his right.

"So *this* is what you do when I'm away!"

He sloppily straightened himself but still said nothing. Half-Naked-Girl gasped with horror, terrified as she watched Luke's nose spray the walls with blood. His feet scuffled clumsily to find the floor, but he couldn't haul his six-foot-three lump off the cushion. From the corner of her eye, Kai saw Half-Naked-Girl wriggle her bare flesh into a pair of knickers, grab her clothes and head towards the front door.

Kai got there first, stood in the small hallway and guarded the only escape. Shaking, the girl finished dressing in the doorway of the dark kitchen. She looked to Kai, yearning to pass through the front door, fearing for her life. Through despair, she turned into the kitchen at a loss for how to leave. Kai couldn't wait all night and deposited one last clout to the side of her head. The girl let out a scream-type gasp, cowering to the expected battering. But the onslaught didn't come. Kai rushed back into the living room and released the rounds on Luke instead. She was so enraged, she didn't hear the front door open as Half-Naked-Girl fled the house, whimpering.

Kai raced up the stairs to get what she had come for – the canvas she had left in Luke's bedroom. As she reached the doorway to his room, he was bounding up the stairs behind. He startled her, wrapping his arms around her body, forcing her forwards onto his bed with his sixteen-stone weight. She quickly turned her face to the side so she could breathe and used her strong back muscles to round her upper back so he couldn't crush her chest.

"I'm sorry, I'm sorry …" he repeated. "Don't go …"

What is *it with these guys?! Dumb* and *ridiculous!*

She struggled and wriggled an arm loose, writhing beneath him to try and break free. On the side table, she spotted the Lovers Candle she had bought him for Christmas a couple of months before: a man and woman, bodies entwined, beautifully carved out of wax. Bucking underneath him, she inched their way over to it, Luke still on top of her.

"Don't leave me, don't leave me," he sobbed. He had buried his head in her neck, too steeped in guilt to see what was happening. Her hand reached out to grab the candle – wavered and missed. *Just a little closer. Damn, he's heavy!* She tightened her abdominals, used her wavering hand to push into the bed, flipped her back upwards and shifted with his weight over to the direction of the candle. She stretched her arm again, seizing the candle firmly, swung it up and backwards behind her, blindly aiming for his head.

The loud crack forced Luke to release his grip. She turned around to see him clutching at his skull. The Lovers Candle had broken into two pieces and lay motionless on the bed.

Kai dived to the floor, snatched the canvas and ran down the stairs two at a time. The front door was still open; she made it to her bags but *where are the keys?*

Luke caught her arm and shut the front door at the same time. He spun her round to face him, placing both his hands on her shoulders, pinning her upper back to the cupboard. Stooping, he lowered his face down to her level, his drunken, teary eyes pleading with hers to hold his gaze.

She looked at the desecrated sofa where he'd sat with the girl, desperate to erase it from her memory. But its wrinkled emptiness confirmed the event had already taken place, as flashing torturous images were beginning to process. Only a patch of the crinkled pink leather cushion remained in focus, triggering the foggy horror of the night. She blinked hard and snapped her eyelids open a few times to wake from this nightmare. Her breath gave way; realising that this wasn't a night terror from which she could escape, her soul stopped the mental fight.

The piercing pain finally erupted at her solar plexus. An explosive volcano blasting a hole through the centre of her body, leaving sharp, jagged edges. It sucked up all the blood and energy from her lower body. Luke sensed the surrender and loosened his grip on her shoulders to try and catch her, but her numb legs gave way as she collapsed to the floor. He sat down beside her.

Floods of tears found their way past the rage and burst the dam. They cried together without talking, a splintered energy between them. She wasn't sure how many minutes had passed but knew she couldn't stay in his excruciating presence. She wasn't sure who he was and wanted to get out of his cheating house.

She stood up, collected her bags and walked hurriedly to her car. He was right behind her.

"Kai! Don't go! I'm sorry."

She didn't remember getting into the car or starting the engine. When she looked out of the front windscreen, Luke was standing in front of the bonnet.

Fool.

If he thought he could stop her Peugeot 106, he was about to find out. She put her foot down on the accelerator and watched him roll off the bonnet as she turned the wheel left. She was only in first gear, but *dammit, is that going too far?* She checked the rear-view mirror and saw him stand up. He was fine. Feeling her body come back to solidity, she changed into second gear and turned left out of the close.

Driving through tears and disbelief, Kai felt sick. She drove to her parents' house half an hour away, instead of heading south. She didn't really remember the journey and had no idea of the time.

Pulling up on the driveway, she found the house in the shadows. The last few hours had darkened into a timeless sphere.

Without looking for her key, she knocked on the living room window and rang the doorbell. She didn't like to wake her folks but was relieved when she looked through the wrinkled glass on the front door to see her dad's figure switch the hall light on and let her in.

"Hello, what's happened?" he asked sleepily. His eyes slowly widened as he looked from her white jogging bottoms up to her blue and white long-sleeved hooded sports top.

"What's going on? It's half three in the morning!" Her mum had also appeared in the hallway. "What's happened?" She indicated her jogging bottoms. "Is that blood?"

Is what *blood?* She thought it a weird question, then followed her mum's and dad's gaze. For the first time that night, she looked at herself and did a double take at her joggers. Her clothes were spattered in blood. *Where's that come from? I haven't killed anyone. Oh yes! – his nose.*

"I've just caught Luke with someone," she explained.

*

"Oh my god! That sounds horrendous!" James had taken in the whole story through dilated pupils.

"Yes, it was a long time ago now. It took about two years to get over that. The image of her bare flesh when she stood up haunted me for a long time. I stayed with him for three years after that."

"Really! Why?"

"Not sure – perhaps I needed to learn how to forgive – to understand that I don't need to stay with someone just because I forgave them. In fact, the person you're forgiving doesn't need to be in your life at all. Send them love and kindness to heal their troubled souls."

"But hadn't all the trust gone?"

"For sure. It put the whole relationship into a different perspective. Before it happened, I'd found salsa tapes in his van." She laughed. "Who even knows what a tape is these days? But the point is, we never listened to salsa, it was always house music. Then after it happened, I remembered that for a few Tuesdays before, I could never get hold of him. He'd been going to salsa with her. God knows what he was doing when I was travelling round Italy for a couple of months in the second year at uni! He was supposed to come out and visit but always found an excuse not to."

"I don't know if I could stay with someone after that."

"I don't advise it. I think trust *can* rebuild, but you always feel hard done by, or that they'll do it again … or that it gives you the licence to do it yourself. Then it becomes a game, to hurt them for hurting you. And when you're young, you play games until you win. If it happened again now, I think I'd just walk away. No drama. It changes you. It doesn't make you stronger, it makes you … different."

"In what way?"

"Well, there's nothing like a trauma to help you on your inner travels – perhaps I attracted it in some way."

"What d'you mean?"

"I suspected Luke was seeing someone a few months before I caught him. I used to say to a friend that I wished I could know for sure, and then I'd leave him. But then those feelings went away and I forgot about it. Guess I got what I wished for. Anyway, now that I've bored you with boringness, let's get back to crystals."

"It's not boring at all, and thanks for sharing that with me. Oh, I have one in my pocket." He produced a smoky quartz tumbler. "Good for calming the emotions and helping reduce fear and anxiety. Brings positivity too."

"Just what you need when dining with strange women! Smoky quartz is one of those popular ones I've never got round to buying. I like to buy ones that come with a different description – nearly all of them say they bring positivity and help with fear, anxiety and negativity. I bought larimar the other day for creativity, good communication and tranquilness." She reached into her bra. "It's super spiritual too."

He laughed as they exchanged and inspected each other's amulets, feeling their energy and planting them back into their appropriate places.

"You know?" He leant forward, placing his knife and fork together on his plate and pushing it to one side. "I'd still like you to come over and show you the Cove, no pressure." He signalled to the waitress for the bill. "Just an easy afternoon with green tea and crystal talk."

"Sounds delightful. Yes, I'd like that. Let me pay half for dinner."

"Absolutely not! I'm getting this."

Chapter Fourteen

Kai leant inside her car and reached over the folded down seats for the last of her paintings to hang on Bayswater's rails and felt a smack on her bottom.

"I know that bum!"

Startled, she sprang up from her near horizontal position and almost snapped her legs in half. Dragging the painting by its string in one hand and crawling backwards on the other, she was doing a very good impression of a flailing turtle. Finally, standing upright, she spun round to the half-familiar voice.

"Reuven!" She laughed, rubbing her shins. "What are you doing here?"

"Wanted to surprise you." He bent to kiss her lips hello. "I trade a bit further down."

"Really? You're an artist – wow! That's great – what number's your pitch? I'll come down and have a look later."

"Two three seven – look for the big blue van. Yeah, get set up and wander down in a bit. I love your paintings, by the way. You ought to put your prices up though."

"People don't want to pay the prices as they are," she puzzled. "They wouldn't pay any *more* for them – especially not when they can walk further down The Road and get them even cheaper from someone else more desperate to sell their soul."

"That's the problem with Bayswater! All the artists need to put their prices up to *value* their *work*." He offered his palms to the sky. "People think that they can pay less for a piece of artwork because it's under a tree … if it was in a gallery, they'd pay more than triple the price. Half of them don't even know what they want, let alone that the artist receives next to nothing!"

"I know, right, so silly! There are some beautiful paintings along here. Buyers can meet the artist themselves and have a real conversation, not a few stuffy words that gallery owners mutter just to make a sale." Kai walked to the rails to hang her last piece. "*We* can tell customers what our work is really about."

"Exactly," he agreed. "I enjoyed spending time with you at the club a few weeks ago – been thinking about you ever since. I knew I'd see you again as you said you trade up here, though I haven't made it the last couple of weeks." His eyebrows furrowed, crinkling the skin on his forehead. "What time you packing up? We could go for a walk through Hyde Park and watch the skaters. Maybe grab something to eat?"

"Oh, would love to, yes, sounds good. I usually pack away at about six-ish."

"Let's see how many people are still walking by. If it's quiet, we'll do six; if there's people still ambling by, we can pack away at seven. Come to see me before then, anyway. We can pop to the shop on the corner for a snack."

"Oh, OK – will do. Hope today goes well. See you later."

"Yes." He came closer. "Sell. Sell. Sell." He named each kiss, planting one on each cheek and a slightly longer one on her lips.

She smiled, watching him head back to his pitch, losing him through bobbing heads.

"I see you've made a friend." Sarah crept up behind her, nudging her shoulder.

"Oh!" Kai jumped. "Well, er … yesss, I think I have." They hugged hello and giggled. She had forgotten her neighbours for a moment, caught in the bewilderment of Reuven.

Bright colours were lighting up The Road in Sunday style. After a few "saleless" chats, Kai overheard a girl talking to her boyfriend standing in front of her paintings.

"I just don't know how they can do that with oils. *I* use oils and *I* don't get that effect."

The girl's bafflement oozed sarcasm and doubt. Kai thought about letting it go, but her ego was growing irritated at the derogatory comments from rude ingrates of Bayswater.

"Can I help you?" Kai approached the girl's hard face which bore freckles and small eyes.

"Yeah, I mean, how do you do that?"

Kai patiently explained her process. "Mix it all with white spirit—"

"White spirit!" the girl exclaimed, squinting her tiny eyes, making them almost disappear. Her boyfriend remained quiet, cringing at his gobby partner.

"Ye-ess." Kai nodded with a slow confirmation and a smile, undeterred by the blunt interruption. "White spirit – and then pour it on. You can come to the studio, and I'll give you a lesson. Teach you how to do it. Thirty pounds an hour. A few hours and you'll learn all my secrets." *Not to mention some manners!*

"Ohh, er … no, er, it's OK, fanx." The girl walked her greasy, straggly fair hair away with her boyfriend.

Hmmm ... didn't think so!

Art was probably the only job in the world where people thought it was acceptable to be offensive to the creator's face. And possibly music. Oh, and teaching!

The heat of the day was guiding the crowds into Hyde Park. After an hour of watching non-buyers, Kai took a walk to find pitch number two hundred and thirty-seven.

Copy Painter Chris stopped her tracks. "Hey! How's it going? Did you find the hotel the other week?"

"Oh hi, Chris. Yes, I did – eventually. Thanks for the directions." Her body language said she wasn't stopping for a long chat, but she did manage a hug for his neighbour, Clive.

"Well done on your sales!" Clive embraced her.

"Oh thanks! Yes, got rid of some old stock, feels good to make some space in the studio."

"You gotta do some new ones now, keep the momentum going!"

"For sure!" She took his guidance on board and headed for a blue van. She spotted the huge abstracts from a few weeks ago and walked towards them, hoping to see the artist. Reaching the canvases and noting the pitch number – two three seven – she turned to see Reuven discussing his artwork with a guy in his late twenties. She slowed her steps, taking care not to disturb his potential sale.

"It's ugliness is its beauty," the guy said to Reuven in an American accent. Kai didn't think they were ugly at all and leant against the blue Ford Transit, listening for Reuven's response.

"Yes! Yes!" he agreed enthusiastically, eyes wide and grinning. "Here, have one of these." He handed the American a leaflet.

"Thanks! It was great chatting with you."

"You too! Enjoy your trip."

Reuven turned and greeted Kai. "Hey, how you doing?"

"I'm good. I hadn't realised these were yours. I saw them a while ago – they're wonderful. Bright and magical." Kai moved in for a closer look. "Are they acrylics?" she asked, noticing the price tag at over one thousand pounds apiece.

"Most of them." He pointed to a few on the end of his pitch. "Those are oils."

"I love how expressive they are. They say 'you either like me or you don't. This is how I was created, and I LOVE THE WORLD!'"

Reuven threw his head back and laughed from the depths of his throat.

"Yes! That's *exactly* what they say!" He grinned widely. "How's it going up your end today?"

"Oh my worrrd! Some people are soo rude!"

"I know. Really nasty with it, too, sometimes."

"Silly people. Do you actually get a grand for yours?"

"Sure. A guy pulled up about a month ago and bought ten paintings for his new apartment in Ladbroke Grove. I gave him a good price cos he bought so many – but yeah, took over nine grand."

"Wow! That's great!"

"Remember what I told you … you have to *believe* you're an artist."

Kai *did* remember he had told her that and wanted to know how he made a living through his artwork.

"Can I have one of those?" She held out her hand for one of his leaflets.

"Sure." He placed the rectangular flyer in her palm.

Reuven Kit
Abstract & Surrealist Painter
Glass & Metal Sculptor ...

Kai studied the small square illustrations of artwork set on the black background.

"Oh, you're a glass sculptor too? Wow! Love these huge public glass sculptures." Kai's insides shrivelled away as, once again, she was reminded of dividing her efforts between painting, swim teaching, life-modelling and the chemist.

"Yeah, my workshops are at home in the garden. You could come over and see them and we can paint together!" He beamed.

She loved his enthusiasm; he was zingy. The twists and heights of his glass artworks had the same energy as his fearless brush-strokes – emerging from a deep sensitivity that underlay all artists.

"Oh crumbs! I've never really painted in front of anyone before – well, not since I left uni." Her bowels shivered – *paint* together! Painting stripped you bare – a long, messy process full of false starts, doubt and obstacles.

Reuven had a couple more dimensions to his artwork – glass and (as she looked more closely at his leaflet) metal sculptures. He seemed well-established … which was probably why he kept his prices high for The Road.

A middle-aged couple, admiring red and yellow circles on a deep blue background dripping with lines of green and sprayed white for a cosmic effect, were looking around for the artist.

"Back in a mo." Reuven bounced away to the man and woman. Kai leant against the open door of his cab and watched the small business meeting unfold.

"Are you the artist exhibiting at the Hilton in Park Lane?" the guy asked. He stood taller than Reuven, about six-foot four, greying hair and a kind, deep voice.

"Yes, that's me! Do you have a card?" He handed them a leaflet.

"Yes, we do, thanks." The lady took it anyway, tucking her bleached blonde hair behind one ear with Ferrari Red nails that matched her red lipstick. "We're staying at the hotel and really love *Presence*. We looked at your website and noticed that you exhibit along here, too, so thought we'd come and find you."

"Ah, I'm glad you did! Lovely to meet you. I'm Reuven." He shook their hands, flowing easily into conversation.

"Your work is wonderful …" The lady caught his eye and smiled. "Though we seem to have a dilemma now as we also love this one too." She pointed to the painting of circles and drips.

"Then buy them both!" Reuven burst, bright like the colours of his artwork.

The couple looked at each other, the lady nodding in exuberance.

"Would you do a deal for two?" the man asked, infected by Reuven's passion.

"*Presence* is one thousand five hundred, and *Messing About* is one thousand three hundred – so two thousand eight hundred. I can give you ten per cent off, so that's …" Reuven looked to the sky and moved his lips to methodically work out the equation. "Two thousand five hundred and twenty pounds."

"That's great! We're flying back to the States on Wednesday, so is it possible for you to arrange delivery – is that something you can do?"

"Sure, I'll add postage and packaging. Let me take your details – do you have a card? I'll give the courier company a call to find out exactly how much it will cost. You can make a bank transfer now for the paintings – or are you paying cash? Then once I've spoken to the couriers tomorrow, you can pay the packing and postage into my account."

"Sure." The guy reached to the inside pocket of his jacket, found his brown leather wallet and slid out a handful of notes. "I have fifteen hundred here in cash, and I'll transfer the rest in a moment." He licked his thumb and finger to casually count through the notes then handed them to Reuven. "Double check it. Here's my card too." The man pulled out his phone to log on to his banking app, and Reuven disclosed his bank details so the man could transfer the outstanding balance.

Reuven calmly flicked through the notes and confirmed the correct amount, opening his own banking app to check payment was complete.

Kai followed the natural flow of this transaction. Reuven's confidence made it look easy. Closing the deal and politely ending the encounter, he walked to Kai.

"Ohhh! So *that's* how you do it! You didn't even take a deposit, just asked for the whole amount upfront."

"Of course! When people buy goods in a shop that are to be delivered, they don't leave a deposit, they pay for the whole lot *and* the delivery as well. Why should it be any different here? Especially as I'm sending them abroad – there's a lot of work involved buying the packaging and wrapping them up so they don't get damaged; asking for a ten or twenty per cent deposit isn't worth it – and if they change their minds, that's a complete waste of my time."

"I suppose. Still – that was all very trusting. How do they know you'll send the paintings? You could have four holidays with that money."

"They'll trust me alright." He laughed, handing her the business card. She turned it over, squinting a little and holding it away from her eyes to let the light focus the letters. *Adam Lukeson, Attorney ...*

"Ohhh myyy! Yes, they'll know how to get hold of you, for sure!"

"And I love your idea of having four holidays on a couple of grand!" He grinned. "We think alike. Greece or Italy is good. Can usually get some good deals after the school holidays. If you sell some paintings, we can book somewhere. I went to India last year over Christmas, planning to go again this year if you're interested? You'll only need about a grand, including flights."

"Oooh – would love to see India. A grand sounds OK." She conveyed the words coolly, but honestly wondered where on earth she would find a thousand pounds in three months. The pit of her tummy began its familiar churn.

"I plan to leave around the middle of December and come back end of Feb. Let's get some lunch."

The mention of food stole Kai's focus.

They weaved back along the pavement so Kai could get her bag, stopping to look at artists' work along the rails and having a quick chat. She was about to introduce Reuven to Clive and

Chris, but they had already met – Clive as friendly as always, and more of a frosty nod from Chris.

As Kai's paintings came into view, she spotted a man wearing a red baseball cap standing at her pitch.

"Oooh, you have a customer!" Reuven chirped in glee. "Go on, I'll wait by your car." He headed to the front passenger side, leant his bottom against the car and crossed his ankles.

"Hello," she announced her presence behind the man, even more nervous than usual.

"Hi!" The man turned to face her and smiled, demurely dipping his chin as though hiding in his cap. Kai bent her head to get a proper look underneath the flap.

"Oh, Vincent!" She blushed, praying that the sound of the traffic would muffle this conversation. "How are you?"

"I'm good, I'm good, thanks." They didn't kiss hello or hug. "I went to visit your exhibition in Raselberry, great paintings. I bought *Volcano* – for my bedroom. The size is great, will fit above the headboard."

"Oh wow!" She considered changing her standing position so Reuven's eyes could stop burning a hole through her back, but that would open her face to his, and she didn't have his confidence when chatting to strangers. Not that Vincent was a complete stranger, and the awkwardness wasn't that both of them had seen her naked. It was more that the conversation with Vincent was now not going to flow freely as she was being watched at trying to make a sale. "Sounds great – you must have a pretty big bedroom!"

"It's a decent size." He laughed. "I've arranged a van to pick it up when the exhibition finishes. I'd love you to come and see it. Come in for a tea or coffee."

"Would love to," she heard herself saying. She guessed she couldn't really turn clients down on the offer of coffee.

"Or if you're free now, we could get something to eat?"

"Oh, er …" She turned to look at Reuven who had his eyes intently rooted to her. "I'm just about to get some lunch."

"Oh, I'm sorry." Vincent seemed embarrassed. "Maybe another time. I'll let you get on. I'll let you know when I pick up the painting?"

"Yes, do – that'd be great." She watched Vincent walk away and turned to Reuven.

"Well?" He grinned. "Did you make a sale? Is he coming back? What did he say?"

"He's actually bought a painting from the exhibition in Raselberry. So, yesss, I guess I *did* make a sale." She opened her car door and took out her handbag.

"Oh, he's local? He didn't say much."

"He's kind of local. I met him at the club."

"Oh, really?" Reuven's eyes widened. "Should I be worried?"

"Definitely not! Come on." She spun him round by his arm. "I'm starving."

Chapter Fifteen

"Oh wow!" Kai exclaimed, truly admiring *Volcano* above Vincent's wooden headboard. "It looks amazing." It was a little oversized, the top edge a millimetre away from the ceiling and the bottom dropping forty millimetres behind the oak wood headframe, but a stunning piece of work. The spectrum of reds were flung to life by the cream background of the walls.

"I love it," Vincent declared. "I pulled the bed forward away from the wall so it could fit. Do you want tea or coffee?"

"Ah, I don't drink tea or coffee. If you have a green tea or hot chocolate, that'd be great. If not, a hot water's fine."

"Oh! It will have to be a hot water then, sorry." He walked to the kitchen, and Kai followed his stiff steps. The black granite worktops sat above pine cupboard units. The chrome oven and microwave matched the chrome dishwasher which coordinated with the chrome washing machine that synchronised with all the chrome user-friendly handles.

"Oh wow!" Kai walked through the harmonised kitchen to the huge window. "So much light. Great view too."

"It's the highest plot in Capes Village. You can see right over to Oxton from here."

"Oooh yes, I know Oxton. What are all the cranes?" She turned to look at him. "What are they doing over there?"

"They're having a sort of clear-out, trying to clean it up a bit and get rid of the locals." Kai remembered the locals … it wasn't such a bad idea! "They're in phase three; think there's about six phases altogether." He filled the kettle and circled it around on its stand until the nodule slotted into the hole. "Do you remember the shops?"

Kai nodded.

"Half of them have gone and they've built new ones."

"What? They've just knocked them down?" Kai was slightly bemused – it was like an ethnic cleanse but the other way round. "Where have they all moved to?"

"Abbotts Head."

"Oh crumbs! That's nearer my way!"

"I know." He laughed. "They have to put them somewhere." He was right, of course. These people were not as fortunate as some to have had an education, or even a job. They escaped into bottles of alcohol and the empty promise of drugs, puked and pissed in doorways and blamed the whole world for their lament. "We can take a walk in a bit and have a look if you like?"

"Yesss, that'd be great!"

He poured the hot water into a mug, made his tea and brought the cups over to the table where she stood. He moved in an unbalanced way and placed the drinks down artlessly.

"So tell me more about Prelude," Kai prompted, taking a seat.

"I started as a sales rep about ten years ago, selling office furniture for people who need a more comfortable and joint-friendly way to be at work. Then later I realised how I could help improve the design." He held up his right hand and made a fist. "That's as far as my wrist will bend." It didn't move a millimetre.

"Oh my word! Has it fused?"

"Rheumatoid arthritis. I've had it since I was eighteen. The doctors said I wouldn't be walking by the time I was thirty. They were wrong. I also had a hip operation when I was forty. Still struggle up and down the stairs, just gotta take it slow. Anyway, have you seen the news—"

"I don't watch the news," Kai jumped in. "I don't watch TV – I don't even have a TV anymore. And if I did, I *definitely* wouldn't be watching the news!"

He didn't seem impressed. "So how d'you know what's going on in the world?"

"Because people love to tell you what they think about what's happening in the world – when in fact, all they are doing is regurgitating what they've been brainwashed into believing."

"Actually the BBC is known for being the most accurate," he scoffed.

Kai rolled her eyes. "And *that's* one of the things people believe because someone on the television has read it off a piece of carefully scripted text. A belief is something we've been told but haven't challenged. It happens all through our lives from the moment we're born. Our parents impart their knowledge, then school does a good job of institutionalising our brains, the corrupt church makes you believe there's a hell where you will end up if you do wrong – and everyone just goes along with it. Because they've forgotten how to keep mental space."

Vincent's jaw had slightly dropped, and the incredulous look on his face was similar to her dad's whenever Kai slandered the government … or any other set of rules (especially his!).

"So you have no knowledge of current affairs?" he mocked. She wasn't deterred.

"This *knowledge* that you saturate yourself with is spun to people across the world to condition their minds. For example, I saw a clip years ago where the news told of how violence broke out and someone was raped at a party somewhere in London. A few sentences later, they showed an image of Eastern European men standing in a group, enjoying the party. The news fed the line 'these Eastern European shown here, later …' blah blah blah, knowing that showing an image with a story would strengthen what they wanted the country to believe. 'Later' *what*, exactly? The guys weren't doing anything wrong in that clip, but most people without a brain now think they are guilty. All because linking innocent video footage with certain words forms a drama. And people love a drama. It's like watching a soap. They're being sucked in for the next negative episode – they can't wait for more bad news!"

"Well, it can't *all* be lies. Some of it is true!"

"They *manipulate* the truth. Take the guy who shot his girlfriend because he thought she was a burglar …"

"He *did* shoot her!"

"Correct. He did. But the only people who will ever truly know what happened that night are him and her … though she's not here anymore. No one else. You can form an *opinion* about it, but that doesn't mean you know what happened."

"And we're not allowed to have an opinion?"

"Of course you can have an opinion – but have you noticed that people who are strongly opinionated are very angry? That's because other people don't agree with their opinions."

They finished their drinks in a prickly silence.

Kai studied his white freckled skin and round face. He didn't appeal to her sexually, and it was clear her views were too bubbleheaded for him. His rigidity reminded her of her dad. Straight. Conservative. And mentally inflexible. Well … *physically*, too, but that wasn't his fault.

"I bet you're a Virgo." Kai took a guess, picturing her dad's study full of messy papers and his reluctance to throw any piece of tat in the bin.

"I am!" He laughed.

"And you listen to the news countless times a day and can't go without watching it?"

"I do. Though I need to know what's going on for business purposes as well, to be fair – exchange rates for imports and exports. We have a sister company in Germany too."

"Oh wow! Whereabouts in Germany? My brother's wife is German, from Berlin."

"In Frankfurt." He looked bemused, ready for the next implication.

"You're a hoarder. You don't throw anything away just in case it comes in useful one day."

He roared with laughter, standing up to get his keys. "Come on." As they walked through the living room towards the front door, Vincent paused in front of the leather corner sofa and looked at his plain living room wall. "I might ask you to do a commission here." He nodded to the space. "A triptych – I have something in mind of three different sized panels expanding in width in ratio, moving along that way … one, two, three." He placed his arms parallel and broadened the distance between them on each count.

Panic creased her face at the word "ratio".

"Don't worry." He read her horror. "I've worked out the measurements."

"Oh, thank goodness for that," she breathed. "Come on then, show me the delights of Oxton."

Chapter Sixteen

"So let me get this straight, darling." Molly sipped her cappuccino in their favourite café. "You went to dinner with James? Who sounds wonderful, by the way. Then you visited old haunts with Vincent from the club. How funny he should live round the corner from your ex – very spooky, darling, very spooky. Have they *really* got rid of the old crowd there? And you're going to India with Reuven?" She gasped. "I'm so jealous!"

"Yes. Yes. Yes. And yes. But we haven't booked anything yet. I love that he's an abstract painter. After work at Bayswater on a Sunday, we walk through Kensington Gardens and over to the Serpentine to sit and watch the skaters. Then round to Hyde Park and past Speakers' Corner. People are so silly at Speakers' Corner. There's one guy, think he's from Egypt. He gets sooo angry when he talks. He's there every week – he must have super high blood pressure!"

"Ahhh, I love Hyde Park and going in the pedalos on the Serpentine. I'll come up and see you one week, bring you some lunch and have a look at the artwork. So is Groovy Reuvey your fave?"

“Yes, I think he is. He’s free: no baggage, no kids, no ex-wives or girlfriends in the background, and he can pack his suitcase whenever he chooses.”

“Sounds delightful, darling. Though doesn’t it bother you that he used to be a doorman … in a strip club? Which reminds me – have you heard from the cock?”

“No, it doesn’t bother me as he’s not doing it anymore. I don’t really think he’s doorman material anyway. He’s educated in the art world, not stuck in a boring nine to five – *no offence* – and has an infectious energy about him that makes me feel alive. And I think he’s had some trauma, though he hasn’t opened up yet. And no, I haven’t heard from the cock since his silly apology email.”

“Good, darling! He is bad news with serious mental issues. You can’t fix him.”

“I know. I don’t really want to fix him – it just seems that I meet someone, we get on, then there’s a flaw. I help them work on their flaws, but by then it’s too late and our own relationship has turned to crap and they’re all ready for the next person! When am I going to meet someone who has done the healing he needs and worked on himself so we can start with the same level of awareness?”

“I guess you had your lessons to learn, too, though, darling. And work on *your* flaws – which is why you’re on a higher vibration for *your* next boyfriend.”

Kai thought about this. “I suppose. I guess we’re all a work in constant progress. Anyway, how’s you and Gavin?”

“We’re all good. He’s closing his salon down and renting a chair in a hairdressers in the old town – will be much better, darling. Less overheads.”

"Ah that sounds great for Gavin. Why is everything so expensive in this country?"

"How's it going with the artwork? Have you sold anything lately? Any luck with the galleries?"

"Sold a few paintings at Bayswater. Nothing with the stuffy galleries. Maybe you should go in and pretend you're me – they may prefer the look of you!"

"They're so silly, darling. Your artwork is amazing!"

"I'm beginning to think it's *who* you know. They think artists are dumb. They tell us they love our work but they're not looking for new artists or it doesn't fit their style … when they have a similar style on display. If they loved the work, surely they think they could sell it … so why don't they take it and try? They don't even want to do it on a sale or return basis."

"Perhaps that's why – because it's too similar to other artists?"

"So why say they don't take my style when clearly they do? Or they say it's too exclusive – surely they *want* exclusive cos no one else is doing it! You can't win – it's all complete bollocks."

"It's a tough gig, darling, the art world."

"Well, let's try it. I'll give you some of my greeting cards or paintings; *you* go into the galleries and see what they say. Or you can send the images online, then it comes from *your* email, and they won't see my name on the back of the card."

"OK, darling." Molly laughed. "Let me know when."

Chapter Seventeen

"It was about eight years ago now," Reuven said to the wispy clouds dispersing across the blue sky as he and Kai lay together on the common outside The Witch's Broom pub. "We were together for five years …" he trailed off. "She's an only child and used to having everything she wanted. We got on – at first." He puffed air down his nose and blinked hard. "Why is everyone on their best behaviour at the beginning?"

"Because they don't want to show who they truly are. They're intrigued and besotted at the start – can't wait to chat on the phone all night and can't keep their hands off you. They don't check out other girls *or* guys. They want to kiss in public like you're the only two that exist – and when I say *kiss,* I mean they *really* want you."

"Like this?" He turned on his side, leant up on his elbow and put his mouth close to hers. He hovered there for a moment and looked through her eyes with his soul. Their parted lips touched but didn't kiss yet. The sides of their noses brushed lightly, producing an electric clench in Kai's tummy. Reuven's heavy breathing sent his lips pressing down, and he kissed her like he really meant it. They closed their eyes, lost in the swirl of desire.

"Mmm ... *exactly* like that."

Reuven eased his shoulder blades back onto the grass and held Kai's hand in the space between. Folding his other arm behind his head, he stretched his legs.

"She was seeing someone for the last two years of our relationship," he continued. "I had no idea until the very end – or maybe I did and just didn't want to believe it. I really only had my brother to talk to at the time."

"Oh crumbs! That's horrible. Thank goodness for your brother."

"Yes. Thank. Goodness. For. My. Brother," he repeated slowly. "She never believed in anything I did, especially not the artwork, and she hated me working at the club. But I never cheated. That's one thing I don't understand. I mean, if you're not happy, then leave. A lot of people can't be on their own; they swing from one branch to another and never spend time to heal and know themselves."

"That's true. But it usually takes some kind of trauma for people to get to that stage ... if they ever do in this lifetime. What you don't learn this time round, you come back to figure it out. Buddhists believe there are seven reincarnations – I really hope I'm on the seventh!"

He laughed and squeezed her hand. "She never believed in anything like *that* either. Not a spiritual hair on her head. But Maz had her own qualities ..." He drifted off with the clouds again, thinking of the good times, wondering how they could turn so sour. "In the beginning, she supported me by coming to all the art exhibition previews, encouraging me to paint – and when I sold, she was happy. When I didn't sell anything, she became nasty, telling me to give it up as no one wanted to buy abstract art … or any art for that matter, and that all artists were the same."

"The same?"

"Cruising through life without doing any *real* work. Her own business really took off – she set up a dance school for kids – and she worked as a PA through the day, and a couple of nights a week she was a receptionist at the club where my brother and I worked the door. That's how we met."

"At New York New York?"

"Aha no, at a dance club called Area. My brother never worked at New Yorks."

Kai listened intently.

"She gave up the reception job but always made me feel that painting wasn't a career. She wanted me to give up being an artist and the door work to get 'a proper job!'" He whined the overused phrase. "I would never give up painting. Not for her or anyone else. I could sense she wasn't happy and tried talking to her, even suggested couples counselling, but she was so against it."

"So you felt backed into a corner?"

"What could I do? I carried on hoping it would sort itself out. She started talking about having children, but I never wanted kids. She knew that from the start. Then, weirdly, things started to calm down. We grew distant but at least we weren't arguing. She let me paint and work the doors, accepting my life – a totally different person. She wasn't exactly *nice*, but she wasn't being nasty either. We just rubbed along."

“Oh. How strange.” Kai wanted to ask what happened next but let him lead as he was in full flow.

“One afternoon, after training with my brother with a few of the lads at his house, I came home to have a hot shower. In the bathroom bin was a pregnancy test half wrapped in tissue. It was positive.” He paused and swallowed hard. It was a long pause.

“You’re a daddy?”

“I’m an *uncle*.”

Kai furrowed her brows, puzzled, then lifted them as high as they could rise. “Oh crumbs!” Her eyes widened as she hoisted her head and shoulders off the grass to face him. Her hand gently let go of his to prop her head, and she wrapped her other arm around his waist.

“He was seeing a hundred girls at the time.” He turned to look at her. “He had no one special. Maybe it was my fault. Maz and I had grown so far apart that our relationship wasn’t physical.”

“So you knew it definitely couldn’t be you. How did you find out it was your brother?”

“She admitted it when I asked her about the test. I didn’t approach her straight away as I was too incensed; thought I may catch her out with texts, or she’d slip up. After about three weeks, I couldn’t keep quiet anymore, but strangely, the anger had been dwindling. Giving it some space allowed me to process it all, and when I finally asked her, bizarrely we both felt relieved. We were done.”

“Sounds like she *wanted* you to find out. I mean, leaving a pregnancy test wrapped in a tissue in the bin? If she didn’t want you to know – that test wouldn’t have been anywhere near the house!”

"Possibly. I wasn't sure who I felt more hard done by: her, my brother, or me." He smiled. "Like I said, it was years ago. It took a while and a lot of self-enquiry, but I have forgiven them both, and me, and have moved forwards."

"Oh. So you're all friends again?"

"Definitely not, but we keep it civil for the sake of littl'un. I forgave them for my *own* sanity."

"And what happened to, er … littl'un?"

"Al is a super charged boy, full of spirit. He lives with his mum, though they have a live-in nanny as Maz works full time. I see him every week and enjoy having a nephew, despite the circumstances. It's not his fault."

"And does Al see his dad?"

"Yeah, he sees his dad every Thursday night. He's a useless father, can't commit to any other evening just like he can't commit to a relationship or anything else. He's so private, too secretive, half the girls he meets don't even know he has a brother let alone a son. He would meet a different girl at the clubs most nights, and I've never known him to have a steady girlfriend. But give him his due, Jay has never missed a Thursday night in eight years."

Chapter Eighteen

"There must be a *hundred* guys called Jay, darling – or Jason," Molly soothed, as they sat on the swings at the local park.

"Oh, really? How many do *you* know?"

"Oooh now, well, let's see ... er ... *one,* darling. Your twit. But 'Jay' could be short for Jake – or even Jack. Or Ge-ene?" Molly managed to make two syllables of the name Gene, her voice rising on the last, her face crinkling as one does when trying to convince the inconvincible.

"Oh, *purleeease!* Or Ben or Matthew or Herbert!" They fell about laughing.

"But you said it yourself, darling. They have different surnames, so it *can't* be him. And people *are* allowed to be otherwise engaged on a Thursday evening. You're putting two and two together and coming up with five hundred."

"I hope so. That's definitely something I could do without!" They held on to the chains and pushed their feet off the black rubber flooring for a gentle swing.

"How's the swim school going, darling? Bet it's so much more fun, working for yourself."

"Yes, it's great actually. I'm liking teaching again as the kids are learning quicker and we can have more fun in smaller groups. Just preparing for the end-of-term show day, where the parents come and watch. It's the only day they're allowed on poolside to see how their kids have been progressing. So I'm preparing paperwork, badges and certificates, then rebooking for the last five weeks from September to middle of October."

"Sounds like it was the best move to leave Greyton Pools, darling. Good to have the clients' cheques going straight into your own bank account."

"Yes, cheque or transfer. Most people pay online into the business account KAN Swim. No one really knows my middle name unless they ask, but I thought it a good play on the initials."

"Of course! Kai Alicia. How clever," Molly marvelled. "Oooh, darling … I emailed those images of your paintings to The Mount Gallery in Kingsford. They asked if I could bring them in!" She grew excited.

"See? I *told* you! That is *outrageous!* I sent them five images altogether about a month ago, *including* those two I sent you, and they didn't want to see *any*. They're so dumb they didn't even recognise them. They say they take artists from different backgrounds … but they choose those backgrounds very carefully. We've just proved it!"

"So, darling, what shall we do next?"

"Go to the papers and give them a story. We can also go to the pompous gallery owners and say, 'Those paintings are actually *mine*, and you rejected them … you are very, VERY silly!'"

"It's ridiculous that it still happens, darling. I'll happily be a part of the story. And don't forget to add 'you redneck mother effers!' Or …" Molly's eyes lit up as her legs pushed her higher. "We could pretend I *am* the artist, invite the press, and at the private view, I will announce the whole gallery is fake, and that the true artist is here among us – Please welcome … Miss KAI NASSERI!" She lingered on the vowels, creating a cheesy introduction, wildly clapping her hands, wobbling on her swing. "Can you imagine their confusion and disgust? All the cameras will be flashing as you come to join me and take the credit. How glorious!" She giggled.

"Thank you, thank you." Kai thanked the imaginary audience to the right and left, rehearsing the evening, her swing also gaining momentum. "It is with great pleasure that I bring to your attention – and to all the artists out there – the bigoted, prejudicial attitudes of gallery owners. I couldn't have done this without the diligence of my secret art agent, Molleee Morgaaan." Her hands opened out to Molly. "Do not be fooled by making great art, it's *who* you know, not the amazing art you slave to create. The latest response I've had is 'Sometimes, we cannot give a reason why we haven't chosen your artwork.' How pathetically arcane!"

"More like complete bollocks, darling. At this point the crowd throws vol-au-vents at the owners, and a food fight ensues. All the paintings are spared, of course, and the press gets a lovely shot of the owners quite literally with egg on their faces."

"Slipping on fresh cream, desperately clinging on to one another, hands shielding their frightful faces from the flashes. They will no doubt be sued and shut down immediately. Hah!"

"*Carry On Cocksuckers!*"

Kai and Molly roared with laughter, clutching their sides, gasping for breath. Tears trickled down their cheeks as the soles of their trainers clumsily scraped the floor in an attempt to stop the swings, bringing them to a jerky halt. Folding forwards, they crumpled to the soft ground, without a care who was watching.

Eventually, they opened out on to their backs, spread their arms wide and surrendered to the ghost-like clouds caressing the blue sky.

"What gives these galleries the right to exploit artists anyway, darling?"

"Their ridiculous overheads, I guess."

"But if that's the case, why don't they reduce *their* commission? They're already screwing the artist by taking fifty per cent. Don't buyers understand that they can buy directly from the artist, at half the bloody price?"

"Yes, but the buyers think that a painting must have prestige if it comes from a gallery, and some even like the fact that they are paying way over the odds. Gives them status."

"Surely an artist has prestige from the great quality *work* they create and sell. It doesn't make any sense. A good painting is a good painting – whether they see it in your art studio or a gallery – it's the same bloody painting! People are daft. Wouldn't be such a bad thing if the galleries went out of business; buyers should buy from the artist. What are they afraid of? Meeting the painter, having a great conversation getting to know them and what they're about; seeing their workspace so they know they're legitimate, being assured of the quality of the work and cutting out the upstarts who have never painted anything in their lives apart from their fingernails (including the men) – and they probably get someone else to do *that* for them too! Honestly, darling, maybe you should find a dead human body and stick it in formaldehyde! These small-time galleries are just not working for you. The Baker Street and Finchley Road framing shops have sold a few for you, so perhaps try a few more of those."

"Yes, maybe." They sat up as three young kids came running over to take their turn on the swings. Kai and Molly conceded the swing-hogging and headed over to the roundabout, sitting in a triangular section each. Kai leant back on the old, flaky, red-painted bar and placed her foot on the ground to gently turn the roundabout a tiny distance clockwise and anticlockwise, as she bent and straightened her leg.

"Who is this Maz, anyway?" Molly asked, changing the subject.

"I don't know. Someone called Marion, I guess. I didn't ask any questions."

"Poor guy! That really is horrid, darling. So he's damaged goods – you make a great pair."

"Yesss. Sounds like he's done a bit of soul discovery too."

Kai's phone pinged. Pulling it from her handbag to read a text, her hand jerked the phone in the three patterns away from her body as her head moved backwards.

"What's the matter?" Molly asked, familiar with Kai's rituals.

Kai turned the screen so Molly could read it:

WE NEED TO TALK.

Chapter Nineteen

Kai has hired a helper for show day to give out certificates and badges, and make sure each child receives monumental praise and encouragement. The support comes in the form of Caren, who knows the drill and is more than happy to assist. Kai and Caren will give the kids a dripping, chlorinated hug, too, in front of their parents, of course … *crumbs, what has the world come to?!*

"Thanks for helping today." Kai is grateful in advance, unwinding the cover off the pool.

"No worries. You might need to come and help me do mine at Cranes Hall at Christmas – if you're still in the country and not sunning yourself on a sandy beach."

"Oooh yesss, swimming in the sea, catching the rays …" Kai tips her chin up towards the polythene-sky, her face warming in the fabricated heat. "Though haven't got any plans this year … so yes, would love to help you. How was the club on Friday?"

"Really good. My usual client was there with his friend … Vince or Vincent, is it? He was asking for you." Caren lays the floats and noodles on the side of the pool. "Think he likes you."

"Oh golly! That's the guy who bought the painting. Oh, so *you're* his friend's usual blonde!" They laugh. "*You* and *Penfold!*"

"Ahahaha, he *does* look a bit like Penfold!"

"I went to Vincent's house to look at the painting. He's commissioning me to do another one." Kai lays the sinkers and big hoops in easy-to-grab places.

"That's great! So you don't fancy him?"

"Not in the slightest."

Eager voices come spilling into the polytunnel, and children from the first group bustle into the changing rooms, hungry to show mums and dads their skills. As swimming caps shuffle their way on to wriggling heads and goggle-tantrums abate, Caren organises certificates and badges in the clear sleeves to keep them dry.

The first five kids sit on the edge of the pool, feet dipping into the water.

"Two hands on one side, roll over onto your tummies and slide in." Kai is proud of them all. At the beginning of term, floats would pop out from underneath the children's twiggy arms, sending them gurgling under water. Tears would tumble as rigid fingers clawed into Kai's shoulders, stiff with fright. Spidering arms and legs had crept to the top of her head, desperate to keep dry. Bendy front crawl knees would angle their feet too high, splashing over the top, slapping the water on the down phase. But today, it all comes together.

"Good, Ben, fabulous floppy ankles, excellent soldier legs." Ben holds one float, comfortable and strong, under each arm and continues across the pool with the others in his group. He grins at his mum, who is impressed with his tidy leg kick, and sticks two thumbs up.

"Great effort, Grace – catch a fish" – Kai stands in front of the little girl reaching her arm forward – "and put it in your pocket." Kai scoops the water in to her hip. Grace lengthens and kicks her legs behind to balance on the noodle, mirroring Kai's doggy-paddle arms. As Grace nears the side, she looks for her mum who claps with delight.

There is a pleasant hum from the spectators' chatter, and the vibe is smooth and easy. Caren is doing her bit, speaking to mums and dads, prepping the next group with hats and goggles and keeping walkways clear.

"Keep going, Leo." Kai turns to encourage the little boy, who now swims unaided. "Magic goggles in the sea …" Leo squares his face to the pool floor and blows bubbles. "How many fishes?"

"Ten!" he shouts, as he reaches the side. "Ten fishes, Mummy!" he tells his mother who has a smile on her face as big as her son's.

"Oh my word! Great effort, you guys!" Kai is thrilled to see Jack and Emma holding the noodles stretched out in front with straight arms, their legs propelling them forwards. "Steer your spaceships through space, faces in and blow bubbles to the stars." The twins take a deep breath, press their faces into "space" and create bubbles that float to the surface, popping like stardust.

"We saw the stars!"

"How many did you see?"

"Ten million!"

"Wow! So many! Keep the engines going at the back of your spaceships." Kai points to their legs, bringing her arms together and motioning up and down. "And park them on the planets at the side – what planets do you see?"

"Mars!"

"Jupiter!"

The twins excitedly park their noodles with sound effects.

"Whooosh! Piushhhh!"

"And NOW that we're in space, let's float on our backs with the staaars!"

Ben holds the inner edges of his floats, one in each hand, Grace and the twins hold the noodles over their tummies, and Leo floats all by himself. Kai wades over to Ben, places one hand gently under his head, a fingertip under his lower back and instructs into his ear, "Gently press the back of your head into my hand and send your hips up to the moon." When he secures the right position, she asks him to let go of the floats. She senses his hesitation. "And remember I'm right behind you." As he lets go, Kai releases her finger from his back. "I've still got you. Now I'm going to let go of your head – I'm still here, Astronaut-Ben – float with the stars." She softly releases the support behind his head, and he floats for the first time on his own. A big smile creeps along his face, elated with his achievement.

"OK, amazing astronauts, heads up ..." She places a finger on the back of Ben's head to prop him in the right direction. "Bend your knees, and place your feet back on Earth." Ben and Leo are upright; Grace and the twins use the support of their noodles to right themselves.

"We have five minutes left to play," Kai announces, throwing rings and floating hoops into the water. She lets them play for a while on their own, jumping up and disappearing under the water to rescue the rings. They pop up and throw the rings back into the water and watch them sink. Kai helps those who haven't quite made it all the way down to the floor and holds the ring a little higher so they can reach.

"OK, everyone, pick up your rings, and bring the big hoops over to the side." Jack and Emma cheat, retrieving the rings with their feet. "We have one thing left to do …"

"The Hoop of Magic!" the kids sing together.

Kai lifts the red weighted hoop into the water, and the kids are already lining up along the wall, one behind the other. As they pass through the hoop, they dip their faces in the water thinking of one thing they are grateful for and the best thing that has happened to them today. Leo doggy-paddles his way first and makes it through without putting his feet on the floor, face in the water.

"I'm grateful for my dinner," he splutters when he comes out the other side, "and the best thing is my *swimming lessons!"*

"Ahhh, that's *my* best thing too!" Kai agrees.

The others follow. Ben manages a few strokes with a hop in between as he holds on to Kai's hand for support to keep the momentum flowing. Jack, Emma and Grace squeeze through one by one with their noodles, shouting their "gratitude" and "best things".

"Awesome work today, guys!" Kai high-fives them all. "You're all super swimmers. When you climb out, go to Caren who's standing over there with the purple T-shirt on." Kai points to Caren, who waves. "She'll give you your certificates and badges. Well done, guys! Have a magical summer holiday."

"Thank youuu," they chant.

"Thanks so much, Kai." The mums and dads come over to poolside. "They're so confident and happy. We'll send you a message to rebook."

"Ah, you're welcome. I know, I think they really love it! I'll save you a space."

More parents arrive with their kids and take spectators' positions. James sits with the others and turns his attention every now and then to Laura to prove he is watching. Children show off their long, straight leg-kick and arms that clear the top of the water for front crawl. They have mastered turning their heads to the side, keeping one ear in the water on the in-breath and gently sliding their faces back in to blow out. Though most haven't grasped breathing every third stroke, they are neat and tidy.

"Great front crawl, you guys! Freddie and Millie, your hands are entering the water fingertips first – excellent!" Kai high-fives them both at the same time. "And Paige, awesome long straight legs!" She slaps two palms with hers. "And Tommy and Laura! Breathing every third stroke! You guys are incredible!" They get a high ten. Kai announces playtime, throwing in the rings and floating hoops. After a few minutes, she gathers the group to the side, Tommy circling the ring around his wrist like a hula bracelet. "In a moment, find a space, do a star float on your back for five seconds, then take a really deep breath and roll over onto your front without putting your feet on the floor and do a star float on your front for five seconds. Then turn it into a mushroom float for another five seconds. How many seconds are your faces in the water for?"

"Three!"

"Six!"

"Five!"

"Fifteen!"

"Listen again. You're on your back for five seconds – face is out of the water. Then after a really big deep breath, you roll onto your front – face is in the water for five seconds." Kai places all five digits of one hand in the air. "Then do a mushroom float for another five seconds, face in the water." She gives them the visual of her other hand.

"TEN!" they all shout together.

"Awwraaaight! Off you go, find a space."

The children disperse, nailing their star and mushroom floats with a ten-second breath-hold.

"Can we do a handstand?"

"Oooh yes! Can we? Pleeeeease?"

"OK, you can do a handstand and then we can finish with …?"

"The Hoop of Magic!" They jump up and down.

Kai watches as interesting variations of handstands take place. They haven't really learnt the technique properly yet, and scissor legs appear over the top, as others stay submerged. Tommy's and Millie's hands are not even on the ground. In their minds, they are doing a perfect handstand.

As this group is more advanced, Kai allows the Hoop of Magic to drift down to the bottom, as they all "graticise" and "besticise". They end on a high, parents equally charged, and success perfumes the air.

At the end of the lesson, kids jump out and parents catch them in their towels.

"Wow!" James is glad to see Laura is not wasting his money. "She's doing great, thanks. I'll text you to see when you're free."

"She's done amazing this term! Yes, message me, we'll sort something out."

Kai is looking forward to her last group. Xander and Oscar are already sitting on the side, keen to start. Jess irritably stuffs strands of her hair under her cap, Katie's goggles are upside down and Rogan is super excited, telling Kai it's his birthday today and explaining his party plans for later.

Kai waves to Xander's nanny who has a prime spot and seems to be saving two more seats.

"My mummy and daddy are coming today!" Xander is so excited.

"That's great! You can show them your amazing swimming!"

Caren ushers away the previous group, keeping the walkways clear and prepares the A4 sleeves with certificates and badges for this final session.

"Mummy! Daddy!" Xander shouts and waves. Kai turns to wave to the two people who have just walked in to sit beside the nanny. But she freezes.

Chapter Twenty

Daddy?! Mummy?! Kai's tummy takes the pelt of two incomprehensible punches, blurring her vision for a moment. A prickly chill moves up the back of her head, the way a horror movie crawls the scalp. *Mummy's* bewildered stare is soaked with guilt and trepidation.

Kai clutches her stomach with one hand as the other grabs the pool's edge to steady her feet – *is the floor moving?* She centres herself, aware she has one more session to teach and five excited children who can't wait to get started. Other parents begin to notice the awkward delay and Kai senses their covert curiosity. She waves to the two slightly late arrivals so as not to disappoint Xander but turns away immediately without waiting for their response. With complete composure, she opens the last session and springs into the pool to instruct from the water – saving the humility of walking past Xander's parents.

"Why are you in the water with us?" Oscar laughs.

"Because it's our last day and we can all have a race at the end!"

"Yesssss!"

"Coooool!"

"Wohooooo!" they all shout.

With fins on, they warm up with front and back crawl, followed by undulating dolphin legs, on and beneath the surface and sideways.

"Now let's take our fins off and swim one length of front crawl. Breathing every third stroke." She demonstrates while standing in the water. "Look to the side to breathe in – this ear stays on the water, long straight leg-kick." She reinforces her words with her arms.

Jess, Katie and Rogan go first. Their body position is just right, they all breathe in to the side, keeping one ear on the water, and make it to the other end of the pool without putting their feet down. Oscar and Xander are next. Their stroke is strong and neat. They compete with one another and reach the end at the same time.

"Awesome, you guys!"

Oscar and Xander high-five each other, bouncing up and down. Their "finless" back crawl is fast, and Kai stands at the other end of the pool to stop them banging their heads. They swim an untimely breaststroke, but it doesn't matter – parents are cheering and full of smiles.

As surface dives turn into handstands, Kai watches Xander reach the bottom and wonders how his father had kept him a secret for eight years. Reaching the sinkers off the side, she throws them in.

"Now, super deep-sea divers, go and find the jewels from the sunken ship, and show me the sparkly treasures when you come up to the top. Altogether, off you go!" Kai stops herself from turning around to look at the two people Xander calls Mummy and Daddy.

Maybe it *wasn't* them.

Perhaps if she doesn't look behind her, they will disappear.

Katie and Rogan take a couple of attempts to get all the way to the bottom and recover their jewels.

"I got a diamond bracelet!" Katie wears the ring on her wrist.

"And I got a gold watch!" Rogan is thrilled as he lays it on the side.

Jess swims to the top, gripping the side with one hand while the other holds the ring flat to the top of her head. "I found the tiara – I'm the princess!"

"You *are* the princess. Princess *Jess!*"

Kai observes Oscar and Xander retrieving their stick-shaped sinker "jewels" from the bottom of the pool.

"These are for you, Mum! Pearl earrings!" Oscar presents them to his mother. "Your favourite!" His mum looks deeply touched, like she could cry at any moment.

"I found the dynamite," Xander yells as he comes to the top. "The dynamite that sank the ships of treasures!" Kai hears cheers and claps from the two people who sit beside his nanny and feels a stirring motion in her stomach.

If all this is true ...

"Excellent, Xander. You are the Chief Swim Inspector!"

... you are actually my nephew. Come on, come on, hold it together – only a few minutes left. "Time for our race!"

"Wohoooo!"

"Yessss!"

“For real?!” Their energy intensifies, feeling privileged to race the teacher.

“Yes, for reeeeals! So let’s line up all together along this wall. Make sure you keep the space between you.” They all line up, fuelled with excitement. “Hold on – I just need my goggles.” Kai looks to Caren, who dangles them into Kai’s grasp. “OK, Caren is the judge!” She quickly puts them on to hide any tears.

Caren walks round to the other end of the pool, where she can see fairly who will touch the side first. “On your marks.” She raises one arm. “Get set. Go!” She brings her arm down to set them off.

There’s a lot of splashing, and then the strokes begin to level out. Cheers from parents raise the pressure. Kai holds back to let the others pass, making it look as natural as she can. She has an idea of who will finish first and touches the side to join them at the end.

“Jess is the winner!” Caren announces. Applause from the spectators.

The boys seem to handle it well and join in the celebrations.

“We beat you! We beat you!” they shout triumphantly.

“Ah, you’re all too fast for me today!” Kai says. “Awesome, you guys! One thing left to dooo!” Kai picks the weighted hoop off the side, wondering if her voice is wobbling, and keeps her goggles on a little longer.

“The Hoop of Magic!” they scream, jumping up and down. They line up and, one by one, swim through the hoop with their best and most grateful matters of the day. The children climb out on the pool’s edge and collect their certificates and badges from Caren. Kai jumps out, too, for her usual hug from Xander and talks to gathering happy parents, who take their kids to get changed.

There is no avoiding it. Kai hasn't looked in their direction since the beginning of the lesson but feels their harsh presence behind her. She turns around to see Xander showing the nanny his accomplishments. Carmen, sensing the strained silence, praises Xander for his efforts and walks him to the changing room.

"Thanks, Kai," parents chime their goodbyes. "We'll email you for rebooking. Have a great summer!"

"Oh! Yes, thanks – great work this term, you guys! Happy holidays!"

Caren starts to clear up, scooping the scattered noodles and floats to the other end of the pool. "I've got this," she says, allowing Kai to enter an uncertain space with the two adults. Kai nods, closing both her eyelids to say thanks and spins her attention to Xander's dad.

"Did you NOT think to tell me you were coming?" she cried. "To *warn* me at least!" She points to her sister, but she doesn't take her eyes from the man.

"I sent you a text saying we should talk, but you ignored it."

"You sent her a text!" Maria sounds offended. "You *knew* she was teaching our son?"

"I was going to tell you—"

"It might have taken him eight years!" Kai sparks. "You never thought to tell me you had a son … with my *sister*?"

Carmen walks out of the changing rooms with Xander – they both look over at the commotion.

"Excellent swimming, Xander." Caren steps in, steering them away from heated voices.

"Yes, that's the best you've ever swum," Kai, briefly distracted, calls down to him.

"We'll be with you in a minute, buddy," his dad adds.

Xander gives them all a wave as the nanny takes him out to the car.

Kai is overwhelmed with emotions. Where does she start after fifteen years of "sister-blackout"? Too many painful questions with unbearable answers. She isn't sure which upsets her the most: the reopening of old wounds, not knowing that she had a nephew … and missing eight years of his life; Jason's affair with her sister, or – possibly the worst – that Jason is the father of her sister's son! She feels sick.

"How long were you seeing each other behind my back?"

"Two years," Jason replies. "I didn't know …"

"Oh, you didn't figure it out we have the same surname?"

"I didn't tell him about you," Maria interrupts. "I haven't told anyone I have a brother or sister."

Kai is more hurt than surprised. "Well, *Nasseri* is not exactly a popular surname. You're not dumb, Jason. You would have figured it out, that's why you never mentioned me to her."

"*Why* would I tell her about you? There was no *need* to talk about you."

"Look, we should all meet to talk about this properly when we have more time," Maria says, fidgeting. "Xander will be wondering where we are."

For the first time, Kai looks at her sister, her heart alive with sadness, pain and confusion, this enormous torture turning the past controversy into a tiny squabble.

Kai wants to say something more, but her throat is jammed. Jason strides through the awkwardness and Maria follows, walking the length of the pool and out the doors. Kai looks for Caren, but she has already left, leaving a note on Kai's swimming bag.

I'M HOME TONIGHT IF YOU WANT TO CHAT. XXXX

Kai sat for a moment on the low concrete step, trying to make sense of it all. Through the madness, she hadn't noticed that Caren had cleared all the equipment and pulled the cover over the pool. Calm, confident Caren – knew what to do in any crisis.

Leaning her back on the wall of the polytunnel, Kai stretched out her legs into the eerie silence. A patchwork of images flashed through her mind. Unfinished scenes and sentences hurtling from all directions. Familiar faces emerged from the depths, while voices and laughter ripped through the mockery.

She had to get out. Standing, she unzipped her wetsuit and peeled it down over her arms. Vigorously pushing one side down and then the other over her hips, it fell to the floor in a soggy clump. Stepping over the neoprene, she towel-dried her swimming costume and threw her shorts and T-shirt over the top. Scooping up the swimming accessories, Kai locked up, dropped the key at reception and headed for her car, hurtling everything into the boot.

She didn't race home – and had no idea what to do once she got there. Hopefully no one would be sitting outside the house waiting to give foolish explanations.

Who else knew? Mum? Dad? The drive was giving a bit of perspective. She reached home and parked in her space at the side of the house. No one was waiting to pounce. *Thank goodness for that* – she didn't have the energy.

Flicking the kettle on for a hot chocolate, she reached for her ten-inch sage stick and lit it with a match. She tilted the tip of the bundle upside down in the flame and gently blew the end to reveal the glowing embers. As ripples of smoke climbed into the air, Kai wafted the sage around the kitchen, then into the hallway and living room. *May all the energies that don't serve this space be released* ... not that any amount of smoke could make this mess disappear, but it might bring a higher vibration – and a choking sensation at the back of her throat. She opened the kitchen window wide, placed the sage into its pot holder, made a hot chocolate, scooped up her mobile phone and went to sit on the leather sofa.

Knowing Caren would be too busy for a phone call, swamped with kids and paperwork, Kai sent a text instead.

HEY. THANKS FOR ALL YOUR HELP TODAY AND CLEARING UP. THINK I'LL CRAWL UNDER THE COVERS IN A BIT, SO SEE YOU SOON. LOVE YOU HEAPS. XXXX

She called Molly, not knowing where to start, but found her rhythm as Molly's easy nature bestowed direction.

"But didn't you see your sister's surname on the form when she booked him in, darling?"

"No. He's booked under Brown. Xander Brown! Never made a connection to the twit ... there are a billion Browns!"

"Hmmm, I suppose so, darling. What about when she paid you. Isn't her name on the cheque or transfer?"

"No, it's not. She must have transferred money to the nanny – who then paid *me*, as payment is from C. Hurtado."

"Oh, I see. Sounds horrendous, darling – could you imagine if you'd taken him home to meet your family ... or if she'd brought him home to meet you?"

"Crumbs! Hadn't thought of that! But Maria and I fell out around the time I'd met him ... and I wouldn't have taken him home to meet the folks or anyone else. How would I have introduced him? *This is Jason, my on and off fuck-buddy, devoid of any sentiment, responsibility and respect!"*

"Hah! Yes, I see what you mean, darling. Why don't you come over here, or I can come to you? Not sure you should be on your own tonight."

"I'll be OK, just feel like sleeping to be honest." She took a sip of her hot chocolate.

"Yes, I can imagine. How did it feel, seeing her after so many years?"

"I could have done without it, to be fair. I was still teaching, so had to try and keep it together. It was weird – if I'd bumped into her walking down the street we may have been able to have a proper conversation. But it was all out of context: her, Jason, Xander ..." She trailed off.

"Are you *sure* you're OK, darling? You seem a bit too cool about it all."

"I haven't got the strength to fight. I'm good, really. You get on with your evening and I'll shout if I need you."

"Sounds good. Get some rest. Love you."

"Love you too."

Kai finished her hot chocolate, lay on her side and curled her knees into her chest. She stared at the wall and felt nothing.

Her phone silently vibrated. She looked at the screen – *Reuven.* She sighed, then answered.

"Hey," she greeted flatly.

"Hey, how's it going? You OK? You sound exhausted."

"I'm OK." She sat up to give him her full attention through the phone. "Just a busy full-on day." She didn't really want to get into the afternoon's altercations and welcomed the distraction. "What you been up to?"

"I've been painting … and thinking about you. We haven't spoken since I saw you last. Hope I didn't put you off, talking about Jason and Maz."

"Jason?" she startled, the events from earlier too raw to ignore.

"Yeah, Jay, my brother?" The tone of his voice encouraged her memory.

"Jason *Kit*?" she asked, desperately.

"Kit?" He sounded confused, then realised her mistake. "Aha no, Kit is my *middle* name; I use it for my artist's signature – more exciting. Our surname is Brown, but I've never really liked it. Can you imagine … Reuven *Boring Brown.*" He dulled the words. "I'm known as Reuven Kit."

Kai's lower jaw released as though she might say something but left her mouth hanging open. Her shoulders jerked backwards, her thighs parted and the three blinks were uncontrollable. She sat rigid.

"Kai? You still there?"

Her frozen voice box thawed for a moment to clear her throat. "Er … yeah. Yes, I'm still here." She softened her tormented muscles.

"I was thinking, I have Alex for the weekend – perhaps we could all do something together, and you could meet him?"

"Alex?"

"Yes, Al – my nephew."

"Al – ex – ander?"

"Aha no! He doesn't like the name Alexander. We call him Al or Alex, his mum calls him Xander – never liked that though!"

Kai felt dizzy. "I think I may have already met him."

"Really? Where?"

"I teach a little boy called Xander – and his mum is … well, his mum is my sister."

"Aha no. His mum hasn't got a sister – or a brother … Maz is …"

"I guess Maz isn't short for Marion!" It was more of a statement than a question.

"No." He realised her mistake. "Maz is short for …"

"Maria!" they both said at the same time.

"Maria is my sister." Kai stood up, felt giddy and sat down again. "She's been lying to you."

It was his turn to be quiet.

"I just found out this evening," she continued. There was a fast-growing thumping in her chest.

"Oh my god! Are you OK?" He sounded muddled.

"And the guy I've been on and off with for the last fifteen years is" – she took a deep breath – "your brother." She delivered the last two words delicately.

Reuven didn't respond. She tried to listen for his breath but heard nothing. The sound of nothing. Possibly the loudest noise in the universe.

Eventually, he resurfaced. "I'm coming to see you."

"Oh … I, er … well, I was going to hide under the covers. I won't be much company …"

"I'll be there in about twenty minutes." He hung up the phone.

The hammering through her chest continued. Flicking shoulder movements and parting thighs were not going to counterbalance this ludicrous wreckage – but she repeated them anyway. Slowly standing, she walked to the kitchen and took her biggest kitchen knife. The was no hurry this time – she didn't have to save herself. Locking the front door, she climbed the stairs to her bedroom and turned the key.

Taking her A4 writing pad, she scribbled a note. She didn't combat the tears and felt she was losing control as she thought of her folks, her lovely mummy and daddy who had given her everything – their support and love. How could they ever understand? She silently asked for their forgiveness. Her brother, Mikey, who was so far away now that they hardly saw each other – his new life and family would keep his focus. Her best friend, Molly, who had been in her life since they were six years old. Caren, Bayswater, Reuven, therapist Jane, the chemist, life-drawing, James, the club, the kids she taught – none of them could stop her. There was no focus, no way out. A circular pressure tunnelled her vision – the edges dark and heavy.

She rolled up her sleeve and sat on the edge of the bed. Laying the heavy blade flat on its side first, she chose a completely different track on her arm. It was to cross all the other scars from wrist to elbow. She swung her legs up onto the covers to get comfy and tilted the metal.

It glided across the skin. It wasn't quite the "one cut" she had fantasised over, but it was deep and fresh.

Inhaling fully, she felt lightheaded. On the outbreath, she sank back into the pillows and closed her eyes to a blurry ceiling and muffled sounds.

Printed in Dunstable, United Kingdom

82499478R00119